Welcome Strangers...

"Such a wonderful day, Adrienne," Nolga bubbled. "Guess what! There are men in town. Real ones, eligible ones, and with money!"

"Don't tell me they gave you a financial rundown as part of their introduction!" Adrienne laughed.

"Silly, you could just tell, by their clothes and the rooms they took. And they've moved in—they're not just overnighters. That is, two of them moved in. The third is staying at the Bay Motel.

"And what's more," she caroled, "another man came in just as I was leaving..."

"That," sighed Adrienne, "is one too many."

PUT PLEASURE IN YOUR READING
Larger type makes the difference
This EASY EYE Edition is set in large clear type—at least 30 percent larger than usual. It is printed on scientifically tinted non-glare paper for better contrast and less eyestrain.

A Man Too Many
Jeanne Bowman

VALENTINE BOOKS
NEW YORK

A VALENTINE BOOK

A MAN TOO MANY

Copyright © 1961 by Arcadia House
All rights reserved

Valentine Books are published by
PRESTIGE BOOKS, INC., 18 EAST 41ST STREET
NEW YORK, N.Y. 10017

Chapter One

It was spring. It had been spring for ten days according to the calendar, the full page advertisements in city newspapers and the clarion calls of athletic director. But someone had slipped up on alerting the weather.

Winds, having stopped over on snow-covered hills until thoroughly chilled, swept down the lake, screaming derision. Daffodils blanched, and violets hid under quivering leaves.

"This awful climate," moaned Nolga Akars.

Adrienne looked at the flimsy negligee her young stepmother was wearing and closed her lips firmly. She couldn't afford a quarrel this morning. An assistant postmaster needed her wits and steady nerves on a Monday that fell on the third of the month. There would be an accumulation of three days of the heaviest mail of the month: bills, pensioners' checks, social security checks, annuity checks, as well as regular incoming first class letters.

"Well, go on; say it," snapped Nolga.

"You don't have to stay here," Adrienne said absently.

"And just where else could I live on the pittance your father left me?"

This time Adrienne controlled the obvious, "Find work elsewhere." Some day she'd say it. She would remind Nolga she had worked before she married Adrian Akars six years ago. Then she had looked upon this old house and the vast tract of land as security. It had been until Akar's death.

"If you think for a minute I'm going to leave here and let you mishandle my investment—"

Her investment. So that was how she had looked upon marriage. Adrienne sighed. Her father had wanted a son, an Akars, to carry on the line of Akars postmasters who had served at The Oaks since Pony Express days. And that of course was his reason for tying up the estate so there could be no liquidation, no sale of land for ten years after his death. Time for a son to grow up.

There were seven years to go. And there had been no son.

Nolga was starting again. Swiftly Adrienne crammed on an unbecoming hat, shoved her arms into a bulky coat and, glancing in a mirror, at white cheeks and dark unhappy eyes, rushed to the door.

"I won't be home to lunch," she threw over her shoulder, and closed the door on an angry, "You can afford to eat in town."

She couldn't, really. The drain Nolga placed on her salary kept her counting pennies. She didn't know how to handle her; she could only pray some handsome, wealthy man would come along to sweep Nolga off her feet and out of The Oaks.

But who ever heard of a handsome single man coming to town, especially one with money?

She'd better forget Nolga. This was going to be a day. She couldn't be a moment late. The old pensioners would be shivering outside the post office, waiting for the checks that meant fuel and food.

There, the post office was head, a single-story cream oblong, smaller than the bank across the street but more important to most of The Oaks' citizens. And there were the shadowy figures of the old. She could open the foyer doors and let them in out of the wind for their next hour's wait. Few could afford box rent.

She started for the rear door, then swung back. "Here," she pulled a dollar bill from her purse, "how about you kids having a cup of coffee on my Dad? It will give me time to thaw out my fingers."

There was laughter, quavering remarks about Dad Akars and about her fingers; then they trooped down the street.

It was what her father had often done, she knew. And it did take the edge off the strain.

The postmaster drove up as she turned to the clock. "Why didn't you tell me you were walking?" he scolded. "I could have swung around that way."

"Needed some fresh air in my mind," she mur-

anxious face, then looked to one side. There was nothing in it: no check, no letter, not even a card.

Those darned Janes kids, she thought angrily. If they could see how their mother haunts this place—

She wished she dared write a card, disguise her handwriting, sign one of their names, anything to ease the heartbreak of neglect. Of course she couldn't. She couldn't arrange a postmark even were she able to bring herself to such well meaning deceit.

Well, well, here was what was obviously a check from *True Crimes Magazine,* for that crazy writer who lived back in the hills. Not that he seemed to need money. She'd heard he really stocked up with the best of everything on his few trips to town.

What was there about him she didn't like? In the first place he didn't seem to her like a professional, and she didn't know why. Perhaps because he was so different from Ed Weaver, who went about his writing like a businessman.

I think it's the expression on his face when a manuscript is returned, she mused, an odd expression, sort of superior.

The clerk had come in quietly, and slipped into place, was sorting mail.

There, the first class mail was distributed. The inner doors were unlocked and, more rapidly than they had been filled, the boxes were emptying.

"Uh-oh," muttered the clerk, "you take her, Add."

Adrienne looked toward the front window, suddenly deserted by Collier. A tall figure in a cart wheel stood there, pounding on the ledge.

"I don't want her," she muttered back. "Don't tell me her check didn't come in."

"Here's where we get reported again," whispered Collier in passing.

"If she raises as much cain at the insurance office as she does here, I'll bet they hold it up on purpose."

"Nuh-uh," Adrienne squared her shoulders, "it wouldn't be worth a visit from her."

She walked forward, to be met with a volley of abuse. The staff was inefficient, dilatory, obstructive, and she, the woman announced, intended to talk to the proper people about it. She had been lenient thus far, but now she would go so high up—

She paused, and behind her the clerk whispered, "We hope she never comes down."

"—So high," the woman intoned, "the whole district will be shaken up as it deserves."

"Bet she registered point eight on the seismograph," came a whisper.

Adrienne supposed there was a woman like Vena Deere in every post office. Let anything go wrong anywhere, and she would be on the receiving end. There other windows at The Oaks received checks from the same insurance company, but theirs always come in on time. For that matter, even the Deere grocery orders went astray.

There, the tirade was over, the woman stalking out. "One good thing about her," Collier observed; "we've been brought to the attention of higher echelons so often we've acquired a record for efficiency."

The morning wore on. The rural carrier came in, and all three turned to opening pouches and sacks of mail he would carry on north and east from The Oaks.

"Hey, Chuck," Collier said, "we had a complaint on your service. Understand you refused to clean out a mailbox."

"I sure did. I don't own that box. If the guy had any sense, he'd know I couldn't remove anything from anyone else's property without a written notice on each piece."

Swiftly Adrienne worked through a stack of double-paged dodgers, advertisements of a Lakeville drugstore sale. Nice timing, she thought, glancing at one page. Cold cures and vitamins, advertised on the day those who'd be vitally interested had the money to buy.

She thought of Chuck as she worked; the extra service he gave. Back in the hills were people living alone. He honked the car horn as he neared, and they came out to wave, knowing if they ever failed to appear he'd drive in to investigate.

"Makes us know we'll never lay sick or with a broken leg for long," one elderly man had said.

"Like having a son care if I live or die," an old woman had confided.

The carrier went his way, the postmaster went to the bank, and Adrienne tackled a bulky bag.

Among other things were two large envelopes. Adrienne slipped a notice into one box at one end of the front tier and one into a box around the corner, whispering, "And never the twain shall meet." She wished they might. She wished she could do something about it.

A lonely schoolteacher and an equally lonely widower were taking an identical correspondence course in metaphysics. How they would enjoy each other's company. Too bad a post office could not put in a computer to pair off kindred souls.

"Psst!"

Adrienne swung toward the window. Little Miss Pinderson was beckoning. "Did it come?" she whispered.

Adrienne nodded, slipped a magazine from beneath a stack and carried it to the window, carefully avoiding a glance at the lurid cover. Instead she watched Miss Pinderson clutch the magazine to her before stuffing it into a bag, then trot off, her eyes bright with anticipation.

For a moment Adrienne watched.

"Miss," a masculine voice, and a hand rapped on the ledge.

Adrienne turned and stared. Tessie would have cried, "Wow." For here was a man, and what a man! But he couldn't be eligible; he simply wasn't the type. Someone somewhere would have stamped him "Hold" and added, "For eternity."

What was more astonishing, he was actually looking at her, appraising her. And he was turning on the charm.

"I want to rent a postbox," he said.

"Business or personal?"

"Oh, very personal."

"Your name?" She hoped it was complicated so she would have a reason to ask him to write it. Handwriting revealed a lot.

"Jones," he stated. "Craig Jones."

Adrienne laughed at herself. Anyway, he was just a little too old for her, wasn't he? And probably he was married. If he were not (she cast an appraising glance at his suit, topcoat, hat, all of the best.), he might take Nolga off her hands.

He was staying at The Oaks, at an inn not too far from the lane leading to the Akars place. He supposed a special delivery would be delivered there? Sometimes he received rather important mail.

"Brokerage business," he said, and Adrienne nodded. That covered a lot of ground. It also seemed to fit. His grey eyes didn't seem to be missing anything. He looked like an alert opportunist. Yet, if so, what on earth was he doing in such a place as this?

She showed him his box and wrote down the combination, gave him a written record of incoming and outgoing mail times (at his request), also the weekend hours on which the outer doors would be open so box holders could pick up any mail. And then he was gone.

At noon Adrienne scuttled out into a cold drizzle. Wistfully she thought of the days when her father would drive home in such weather. She'd have a fire going in the kitchen fireplace, a hot lunch, and they'd spend a cozy hour watching the wind-whipped waters of the lake and feel secure in their warm home.

Now she settled on a stool and ordered a sandwich and coffee and felt worse than usual because she was sitting where she could see herself in the mirror on the back wall. She looked shabby, shaggy. She should do something about herself, but what could one do without money?

She returned to the post office and looked on the grilled windows as bars of a prison. And she had served only three years of a ten year sentence.

And then she looked again. Another man, another strange, young, good-looking man, had appeared at one window.

Perversely hope sprang up. If this kept on, if enough eligible strangers appeared, she might break out to freedom.

"I want to rent a box," said the young man as Adrienne stepped up.

Chapter Two

Adrienne studied the young man as she made out two receipts. For he had asked for a second box, a large one.

He wasn't as handsome as Jones, she decided, writing down the name of Rodman Burrows. He was designed in squares: square hands, square chin and a square brow under the soft hat pulled so only a rim of sandy hair showed.

His eyes were grey and completely opaque. Why, he didn't even see her. To him she was a robot installed by an efficient government and responding to vocal impulse.

"Would you like me to write down the combination?" she asked.

"Just tell me."

"Once around to eight and a half, back to six and a half and stop on five, for the personal mailbox."

Adrienne shuddered at the next, but there was nothing she could do about it. "Once around to eight, back to six and a half, and stop on five and a half."

She looked up, firmly believing she'd heard a

15

click in Burrow's mind; a click like the closing of a filing case.

He stepped back to read the mail bulletin, and Adrienne would have taken an oath that each letter, each numeral was indelibly printed on his mind.

But she doubted she was. She hadn't registered on his mind as a human being, much less as a girl.

And she was furious. There had been a time when she hadn't been able to walk down the street of even Lakeville without heads turning. Even on her few trips to the city men had taken at least a second glance.

Burrows walked off; Adrienne watched but thought of herself as well. When had she started to slip? Since her father's death? No, it had been earlier. Why?

There, the man had walked into the pelting rain, had made a dive into a car across the street and was driving off. Not a particularly spectacular car, but one that rather went with his clothing, of good quality and dark in color.

Sinking into a swivel chair, Adrienne stared out at the rain.

Collier came in and went into a huddle with the money order book, a popular pastime the first of any month, but he didn't disturb Adrienne's thoughts.

She was tracing back, and now she knew the answer. She had decided, six years ago, that she would start saving getaway money. The very moment she had enough to leave, she would go to the city and start a life of her own.

As she finished high school an opening had come on the post office staff, and she, who had worked as an extra during the holiday rush, was hired as a clerk. Later, on her twenty-first birthday, she took her civil service and became assistant to her father.

Why had she stayed on? she reasoned now, sorting the late mail and aware of a cart wheel hat hovering near a window.

In the beginning, because she hadn't saved enough to leave; later, because of her father's health. In her position, she was able to relieve him of responsibility. And after his death she had felt she had inherited the responsibility of Nolga.

Seven years to go. Good heavens, she'd be thirty-one.

She was going to have to be more realistic. Nolga was thirty-five; why should she have to be pampered?

Thank goodness, there was the Deere check. She went to the window, to have it snatched from her hands with an ungracious, "Well, it's about time. And the banks are closed."

"You could have it cashed at the grocer's," Adrienne allowed herself to say amiably.

"And have the whole town know my business?"

She swished out, and Adrienne, returning to

sorting, felt Collier pat her on the back. "Good girl. I'm afraid I'd have asked her why she thought her business sacred when she broadcasts the business of everyone else, with embellishments."

They had just finished the late mail and were going about preparations for closing for the night when the door of a box slammed shut and a hoarse voice gave a chortling cry. A moment later a figure appeared at the window.

Adrienne walked up, wondering why Hobart Hanson was always either the first or the last to come for his mail.

Her memory, trained to be photographic, presented a grilled picture of him: plaid mackinaw, collar turned up, knit cap pulled down over his ears. She supposed riding in a jeep in this weather wasn't comfortable.

But it was the expression on his face which caused her to lose step. A gloating triumph. Oh, yes, he'd received a check.

"How much time have I got?" he barked affably.

"Practically none," she replied, then added, "I can wait a minute or two."

"Good girl. Good wonderful girl. Airmail envelope, please."

When she turned back he was endorsing the check. Next he ripped open one of the two letters he'd received (always two, she thought, and always from the same women, one old, one young).

Now he scribbled on one, tore off the scribble and added it to the check thrust in the airmail envelope.

It was then he looked up, found her watching him. "Well?" he snapped.

"Look, you can drop that in the outside box; it will go out as early. I want to get home before it starts raining again."

"Yeah," his anger died, "okay."

She dropped the opaque glass window and hurried. But when she reached the side of the building the jeep was already heading down the highway to Lakeville, not back to town or to the hills.

She wondered about him all the way home. When he'd rented a box he'd said he was "holed in" in an old lumber camp in the mountains. He'd appreciate it if she told no one about him. He'd been trying to find some privacy for months, and now that he had it he didn't want to have to move again.

Stiffly she had replied, "We do not give out addresses to anyone. Our business with people is confined to handling their mail."

Yet there had been times when his mail had accumulated for as much as two weeks, and she had wondered if she should alert someone. Two things had stopped her: her lack of knowledge as to where in that maze of mountains he might be, and his attitude towards privacy.

On his first trip in for mail he had asked if any-

19

one had been looking for him, and when she'd given him a completely blank stare, he'd shrugged, "I have some cousins who'd like to locate me. Prime moochers. Minute I earned a little money they moved in. They might even try out some other names; names I write under."

"Mr. Hanson," Adrienne had said, "your own mother couldn't locate you through the post office except by mail."

Yet she had felt a certain sympathy for him. She knew something about relatives anticipating and taking moneys earned as a right.

Wonder if he sent that check to a wife, she mused, running, now that a shower had started. Come to think of it, none of those letters carry a return address. And she had never paid attention to the postmark.

Ahead, the old Akars house stood like a child's finger painting, lopsided oblongs of topaz light indicating half the rooms in the place were using up electric current.

Into the kitchen with a rush went Adrienne, then stopped, warily. Logs blazed on the small hearth; a table was drawn up nearby. The savory aroma of food came from pots bubbling on the range.

Then Nolga made her entrance with a, "Darling, you are late."

Adrienne braced herself. Nolga was being one of the Gabors this evening. This could be expensive. She had a new haircut and wave—and oh my goodness! Nolga had thrown off a cotton housecoat and stood revealed in what to her stepdaughter's eyes looked like a space suit: a shimmering one piece suit the color of spun aluminum.

"Such a wonderful day. And, guess what. There are men in town: real ones, eligible ones, and with money."

"Don't tell me they gave you a financial rundown as part of their introduction."

"Silly, you could just tell, by their clothes and the rooms they took. And they've moved in; they're not just overnighters. That is, two of them moved in. The third is staying at the Bay Motel. He's a love, tall, dark and so mysterious.

"And what's more," she caroled, "another came in just as I was leaving. And he," she paused dramatically, "looked like a private eye on a TV-show. Honest."

"That," sighed Adrienne, "is one too many."

Actually it was two, but as the one she hadn't met was stopping at a motel, he could be a transient. The first two were, of course, the two who had rented boxes, Jones and Burrows.

"Don't tell me you met all of them."

"Oh, but I did, all but one. You know the girls played bridge in the hill room today, and we played late, and when we came out, for some reason my bag slipped, and everything that could roll went kiting down those three steps into the lobby—"

"—And the men swarmed."

"Three of them did; the fourth just looked. I was furious. I mean the way that he looked, as though I'd done it deliberately."

Adrienne's eyes danced. "Did you hear something like a click when he looked?" she asked. "Oh, all right, did he wear a dark suit and look sort of square?"

Nolga's eyes dreamed a moment. "He did at that. Just wait until I meet him. I'll bring him to heel. Oh, but think, darling, all of those eligible men and me the only young widow in town. We'll have a ball."

Adrienne looked anxiously at the table, then sighed with relief. It was set for only two. She went on to her room feeling like a debt-ridden husband alerted to new bills by the sudden concern for his comfort.

The two surviving Akars had an hour of comfort. Nolga could cook when she gave her mind to it. She cooked as she dressed, with an excess of seasoning, but she cooked so rarely Adrienne's digestive system wasn't threatened.

The dinner hour was over. The dishes were stacked, and for once Adrienne didn't intend to wash them. She had other more serious matters to face. She dreaded it. This stormy evening with its warmth and food had been a safe island after months of drifting with Nolga's current. And she had to bring it to an end.

Onto the cleared table went a stack of bills, sorted, classified.

"Nolga, this has to stop," she began earnestly.

She didn't get any further. Nolga was voluble. A housekeeper was paid something for her work, wasn't she? And as Adrienne was so stingy with her cash, she, Nolga, had to charge.

"Your father would be ashamed of the way you begrudge me the little I take for looking after you," was her final thrust.

Adrienne heard the patter of her feet, the slam of doors, the rush back downstairs, the front door, and then the car motor starting.

"I'm sorry, Dad," she whispered; "you spoiled her first. There's nothing much I can do; she's older than I am."

She sat for a little while listening to the rain slap the windows, the deep deliberate tick of a clock brought across the plains by the first of the western Akars. And she tried to follow Nolga with her mind.

Ordinarily she would go to some chosen friend to pour out her woes. Tonight, Adrienne wondered if she wouldn't go to the hotel, perhaps, as she's done once before, pretending to have lost something in the crash of her handbag.

Adrienne jumped up suddenly. She might even bring back one of the men she had met.

She didn't. From her room Adrienne saw the dejected little figure slosh back the driveway to the side door and read defeat in the droop of her shoulders. Obviously the quarry had retired early, finding nothing at the hotel to keep them in the lobby.

She supposed it was hard on Nolga to live out this waiting period. Nolga didn't have the inherited love and lore of The Oaks and the old Akars place to make it bearable. Nor had she too many friends. Women at The Oaks were either too old or at that age where growing families occupied their minds.

Then Adrienne came full circle. Nolga could leave. She was free to go to the city and find work and friends, whereas she, Adrienne, couldn't. She had used up her getaway savings.

Adrienne paced the floor until the chill of the room sent her to bed. She'd been over this problem so often; why had it become suddenly acute?

Morning brought a surprise, but a pleasant one. Nolga wasn't down, and when Adrienne checked to see if she were ill, she received a flounce in bed and the drawing up of covers as an answer. The underpaid housekeeper was on strike.

At least, she thought, enjoying her own coffee as she watched a watery sun splash the lake waves with yellow, that's the way she rationalizes. Woman to woman, I'll bet she wants my steam over the bills to die down.

Compared to the previous day, the post office was quiet. A few of the oldsters came in for money orders. Adrienne could have predicted that. A national clothing house had sent catalogues the last of the month advertising spring sales and, more important, a clearance of winter items. Pensioners spent the warm months preparing for the cold.

Adrienne knew the catalogue by heart. There had been two or three dresses she yearned to own, some lingerie, sweaters and a particular pants outfit.

Her mind flashed to the silver sheen lounging suit Nolga had worn the previous evening, and she shivered with apprehension.

Tessie came in to help with the late mail, brimming with gossip. Had Adrienne seen the private eye? She understood he'd spend practically the whole day at the coffee shop's front table, half hiding behind that atrocious paper palm, watching people pass by.

"I do wonder who he is," she mused.

"Wait a moment and I'll tell you," warned Adrienne, and went to the window.

"Box," barked the man standing there.

"Business or personal?" Adrienne looked completely uninterested, but she was missing nothing. This was the dream man Nolga had raved about. Well, let her. To Nolga's stepdaughter he looked more like an actor who had rushed off the set and on to The Oaks without waiting to change.

Dark hair, dark eyes; hair a little too long, eyes a little too tight. Hands? Adrienne watched the one used to scribble the signature. Too smooth. In her lexicon he was too everything, a man too much, a man too many.

Chapter Three

Frank Van De Mark.

He wrote it with a flourish, then looked up.

"Not that I'm expecting much. Like to pick it up weekends. Expect you have a lot of people who do, don't you?"

"They don't give their reasons for wanting a box," Adrienne evaded.

"Folks in hotels, maybe in out of the way places, can't always get in at mail time?"

"The charge is by the quarter, Mr. Van de Mark."

"I should be here that long," he groaned. Then, aware he was insulting a local citizen, "Never lived in the country myself. Doctor says I'd better. Suggested the inn as the quietest place this side of—" He broke off, swallowed. "Said the cooking was right, too. Not too rich."

Adrienne allowed herself a small laugh. "If it's unseasoned living you're looking for, Mr. Van de Mark, you may have come to the right place."

"Well, be seeing you." He withdrew reluctantly, and both girls were puzzled.

"He doesn't look sick," Tessie protested.

"He's thin enough to have an incipient ulcer," Adrienne remarked.

"And if he were a private eye," Tessie continued, "surely he wouldn't dress like the popular conception of one."

"Maybe he's played the popular conception until he's built up tensions."

"Yeah. But imagine three new men, single, within two days."

"Who said they were single?" Andrienne offered.

"A gal can hope," muttered Tessie.

A gal could, but Adrienne couldn't. She had no illusions, and her mirror confirmed her attitude. She was as drab and uninteresting as her life had become.

At the bottom of the mail sack a sheaf of papers had slid out. "You go on; I'll take care of them," Adrienne said, almost adding, I've nothing else to do. "And, Tess, better come early. Collier may not get back in time for the early mail."

Tessie hurried off, and idly Adrienne looked down at the papers, glossy with good lithography. She picked up the manila envelope, which had been torn in shipping.

"Miss Caroline Johnson." She was that mousy little grade schoolteacher. Now would she want these immediately, or should the envelope be patched and returned to the sender for a fresh copy? Were they important enough? Or would the delay inconvenience little Miss Caroline?

"Oh, my goodness," breathed Adrienne, and sank into a chair, "it's the first lesson from a charm school."

Up jumped an illuminated phrase, "Think yourself beautiful. You are beautiful."

Half hypnotized, Adrienne read on.

"Analyze the famous beauties of today or yesterday. What has set them apart, made them memorable?"

She skipped on down to the concluding sentence: "Regardless of how it was started, by parents or by press agent, the individual's own belief in their charm—"

One would have to be pretty much of an egotist, Adrienne reasoned, then saw another line: "People are like plants, like trees or flowers that cheer the eye of the beholder. You owe it to yourself and everyone who must look at you to be the best possible of your specie."

Adrienne had a sudden vision of herself as a very dilapidated plant, bruised by weather, bent to the gale, even mud-splashed, certainly no joy to the beholder.

Reluctantly she stacked the papers together. This was not her lesson. She'd better be thinking up some means of disguising the place where the envelope was broken so Miss Johnson would not be embarrassed.

A final tap on the table, and a sheet slipped out and slithered to the floor. It was meant for her: Adrienne knew it. For there in the *before* photograph was a girl who looked exactly like her and here in the *after* one that she could look like.

"I'll do it" she said aloud, "and right now before I pay bills."

She defended herself. She said, "I must take some action, do something. I can't go on like this for seven more years."

She was still talking when she found herself dialing a number.

"Gypsy, this is Adrienne." She waited a moment, said the conventional things, then with a note of desperation, "Gypsy, have you time to see me this evening? I just have to do something about myself."

Cheerily Gypsy Ladue Duncan's voice came over the wire. "Wonderful. Clive and Clyde are going to a Scout dinner. Why not run up and have a bite with me? No trouble; a couple of trays in the studio."

"Oh, my goodness," Adrienne said, when she finally faced Gypsy, "I forgot to call Nolga."

"I suppose she always calls you," murmured Gypsy, and indicated the telephone.

The buzzing sound of the telephone in the Akars house got no response.

"I can't reach her," Adrienne said at length.

"She's probably still at the inn," Gypsy soothed

her. "She was there around five. Clive happened to mention it. She had introduced him to, believe this or not, a Mr. Smith and a Mr. Jones."

Adrienne laughed. "I believe it. I haven't met Mr. Smith, but I longed for Mr. Jones' name to be unusual so I could see the man's handwriting."

"Calligraphy or graphology?" Gypsy asked.

"I don't know much about either, but I am interested. And with so many hundreds of letters passing through my hands, I suppose I have picked up the rudiments. Not character as much as characteristics seem to show through."

They talked of local affairs while Gypsy prepared two trays, one with dishes and silverware, the other with a casserole and salad.

"I never see you at any of the dances or parties," Gypsy observed.

"A man can go stag," Adrienne said, "but a girl—"

"Don't I know! And I made such a flamboyant wallflower. You weren't old enough to notice, but during my difficult days I found myself wearing the most garish colors when I was on the defensive."

This, thought Adrienne, following Gypsy along a covered breezeway to the studio, was what she enjoyed about Gypsy. Without pretense herself, she allowed everyone else to be truthful.

The big studio blossomed with low lights, came

alive with flames leaping up the big chimney of the fireplace.

Adrienne sank into a deep chair, sighed deeply and relaxed.

"You don't know how I've been looking forward to this," Gypsy confided, arranging plates on low tables. "I judge from what you said when you telephoned you want . . . pruning?"

"You've been looking forward?"

Gypsy waited a moment, dark eyes staring at the flames. "How would you feel if you were turned loose in a post office with everything in the wrong place? Wouldn't you want to bring it back to order? Or a garden—I know you do the gardening at home. Your choice of color and line—"

"You would see people that way," Adrienne agreed, "and want to do something. Why did you never tell me?"

"Dear child, I couldn't. I might have fixed up the outside, but your desire had to come from the inside before there could be any real change."

"But, Gypsy, I've always wanted to be different. I just didn't have the money to do anything about it. I haven't now. I'm going to have to pay you a little at a time."

The story poured out then, right up to the bills still on the breakfast table as far as she knew.

Then, like a dash of ice water, came Gypsy's comment. "How cruel you've been, Adrienne. Now wait. You didn't mean to be; quite the reverse. Look at it this way. Nolga is selfish, self-centered. It is a weakness of character, and you haven't done a thing to help her overcome it.

"Suppose her weakness had been alcohol, would you have, though begrudgingly, plied her with drink?

"Adrienne, nobody ever helps another by giving in to his weakness."

She waited. She brought handkerchiefs and poured hot coffee. Then, when Adrienne could look up, she laughed at her.

"Now that the drouth is broken, let's have something to eat. Then we'll plot a new life. Think you have enough intestinal fortitude to stand up to it?"

Adrienne drew a deep, shuddering breath and nodded. "Yes. As long as I know I'm helping her as Dad would have wanted and failed."

"Naturally," commented Gypsy, "he found in Nolga the little girl you hadn't been. You'd always been so conscious of his desire for a son, you tried to be what you thought a son would have been to him. For instance, your work. You became proficient in that for his sake rather than your own, didn't you?"

Miserably, Adrienne nodded.

"Fine; he appreciated it. But you can see now how the spoiled darling must have appealed to another side, even while it probably irritated him.

But that's past. We'll look at it only to clear away mistakes so they won't crop up."

There wasn't time to accomplish much that evening. Gypsy made a few sketches, then placed Adrienne before a mirror and deftly showed her how she would look with her hair arranged or even cut differently.

"If you leave it the present length," she confided, "you can have a change of view. I think that is good. Personally, I get very bored when I look at myself day after day always in the same frame."

She gave the glossy black mass a few swift strokes of a brush, swirled it up one side, tied the ends, then tucked them under.

"Why," breathed Adrienne, "I look like a different person."

"Correction." Gypsy spoke through boned hairpins. "You look like yourself, smart, efficient, unbeatable."

Unbeatable. Adrienne carried that thought home. Clive and Clyde, on returning, had turned the car to drive her across town. Caught up in their gay account of the Boy Scout dinner, she found she could match their happiness.

"I'll go in with you," Clive said when they found the house dark.

There were signs of Nolga—clothes strewn around, the bills scooped off the table and into the wastebasket, as Adrienne found when Clive offered to build a hearth fire.

"I think I'll go on to my room," she said. But when Clive had left, she didn't.

She wanted to jot down the many thoughts which had come to her.

"When something has got you down," Gypsy had said, "don't sit and mull it over. It grows with mulling. Instead, take action, any kind of action; then you will feel you are doing something to combat it."

Adrienne worked out one line of action. She wrote a notice to each merchant that she would no longer be responsible for anything charged by anyone but herself.

And now she would start looking, planning ahead.

She left the garage light on and went to her room to stand at the window and look across to Lakeville, a twinkling carpet thrown across the lake front, hanging from low hills.

"Whee!" She stretched and breathed deeply. "I do believe I'm coming alive. Bless that stony-faced Rodman Burrows for looking at me and not seeing me."

Nolga came in late. Sleepily Adrienne became aware of voices and laughter, then of several people in the kitchen.

When she awakened again it was daylight, and for a moment she lay wondering why she was happy, why she felt as though some great smothering grey blanket had been lifted from her life.

For the first time in months she took pains with her appearance, wore the one good dress she'd allowed herself that year, a rayon and wool sheath of beige with buttoms the brown of her eyes. Her hair had swept up obediently, and when finally she dug deep into a drawer to find rouge, she was amazed at the difference in herself.

Surprisingly, Nolga was in the kitchen busily making waffles.

"Morning, darling. I tried to reach you last night," she called over her shoulder. "Wanted you to join us at the inn."

"I went calling," Adrienne replied.

"Did you? We—" Nolga turned and stared. "What on earth has happened to you?" she demanded. "Adrienne, surely you're not wearing that good dress to work, not when you wouldn't let me wear it to—"

"But I intend to wear this and others like it, Nolga. It suddenly dawned on me that I was earning enough money to look like something."

"Adrienne Akars, I've never known anyone to cry so often over lack of funds. Don't tell me you received a raise. One doesn't in your job at this time of year."

Adrienne poured coffee and settled down. "No, I didn't. But I did something else. I wrote to all of the merchants telling them from now on I would pay only bills which I personally had run up. I'll take care of this month's, but after that you're on your own."

"Addie, you can't, not at a time like this." Nolga cut short her first wail of dismay to ask severely, "What would your father say to your refusal to share with me as I share with you?"

"He could afford you, Nolga; I can't. I'll prepare my own breakfast after this and have lunch and dinner in town. It will be fun for me, and in that way you won't have to share food. We have equal rights in the house, so the roof is assured, and I'll pay half the power bill.

"The car license is paid, the insurance only until July. After that, as I never use the car, you can pay."

A crisp but almost black waffle was placed before Adrienne; Nolga's small hands were trembling. By the time she was seated across from Adrienne, tears were falling.

Nolga wept like a small child. Tears formed and trickled down her cheeks until only the strong of heart could resist offering comfort.

"I've tried so hard," she began tremulously.

Swiftly, before she would weaken, Adrienne stood up. "Nolga, look at it this way. We've nearly seven years to go before the estate can be settled. I simply cannot go on living this drab life. It's not doing either one of us any good. I can't get away without saving, and I can't save while I'm paying your bills. You resent my being able to do so, and

I'm beginning to resent having to. So I've quit for both our sakes."

Getting into her coat and tying a scarf loosely over her sleek coiffure, Adrienne heard a few muffled words: "You've always hated me because I took your father away from you."

There was a light mail that morning. Collier gave Adrienne a quick, startled glance. "What have you done to yourself? Don't tell me; just keep on looking that way."

And then the window slides went up and just outside the stamp window stood Rodman Burrows.

He looked at her once, a second time, and then he smiled. "Good morning, I believe your sister took care of me yesterday. You are Miss—?"

"Akars. I am my sister," she babbled. "Is there something I can do for you, Mr. Burrows?"

Chapter Four

"Akars," Burrows repeated the name. "Pioneer family here by that name, I understand."

Adrienne nodded. "My father's family."

"I'm interested in the history of this area. Perhaps some day—" he stopped short, puzzled at the sudden change in Miss Akars' expression. Now what had he said?

Adrienne had felt her high spirits plummet down. Just as she had thought she'd achieved recognition as an individual, a rather good-looking young woman, this Rodman Burrows had had to spoil it all. He was obviously another writer looking upon her as a source of information he needed.

"Oh," he seemed to recover, "stamps, please, eight-cent and a sheet of airmail. And would you mind weighing this?"

Adrienne didn't mind at first, but when she looked at the long fat envelope she was indignant. The address had been typed and told nothing about Rodman Burrows other than that he knew some Ralph Edson in Oak Cliff, Texas. And who had ever heard of Oak Cliff?

Yet busily the analytical part of her mind worked. Within this envelope were sheets of the same size, sheets of letter paper, not a folder or a brochure. Who could this Ralph Edson be that he would receive several pages of typewritten matter from Rodman Burrows?

Of course Burrows, who didn't look like Adrienne's idea of a writer, might be doing research for some friend. Yet why would someone in Texas expect someone else to travel to this forsaken corner of the Northwest?

"Miss Akars," Burrows was folding the stamp sheets in their oiled covering, "forgive my bluntness. I am an engineer, inclined to take a direct approach. If you are, as you said, 'your sister,'" his grey eyes were twinkling, "I believe you would prefer that to insincerity."

Adrienne waited a moment, mostly to catch her breath. Then, seeing Burrows turn away, "Wait, please. Why do you say that about my sister, I mean me?"

He was smiling now. "I overheard someone telling how you'd brushed off his attempt to charm you."

That, she thought, would have been the private eye character, and suddenly she joined him in laughter.

"I'd like to talk to you about The Oaks," she said.

"Then can we choose a time and place where

we wouldn't be interrupted? I suppose you have Sunday tied up."

"I'll be equally frank," she returned. "I haven't."

He suggested they drive out some place for dinner, then, seeing people approach, said he'd be in to make final arrangements to meet later in the week.

Adrienne saw him leave, watched him go toward his car across the street, then saw something which caused her to grip the package she'd brought forward to deliver to a Mrs. Caronby.

"Addie," scolded the woman, "why are you staring, and at what?" She turned around, grunted and said, "Your stepmother. My she is having herself a ball with all the strangers in town. Why, I heard last night at The Oaks—"

"There is six cents due on this, Mrs. Caronby," Adrienne reminded her. "As to last night, I was to have been with her—"

Adrienne turned away, missing the last of the tableau of Nolga stopping Burrows, laying a pleading hand on his coat sleeve, lifting her face to stare up eagerly as she asked some favor. Adrienne knew the stance. She wondered a little bitterly if Burrows had succumbed as did nost men.

Evidently he hadn't. By the time Mrs. Akars had crossed the street and faced her, she was in a petulant mood.

"You can't say I didn't try," she charged.

"Try what?"

"To make him come to our dinner tonight. For you. I mean, he was to have been invited for you. Craig just insisted. He said you'd make an ideal couple. What makes it so curious is that he said he'd met you."

"Craig?"

"No, that Burrows man. Addie, why do you look so funny?"

"Natural," murmured Adrienne, wondering herself why Burrows had refused unless, as he'd said, he wanted to talk to her alone.

"Oh, well, you can concentrate upon Dan. He's a little on the stuffy side, too. Of course Frank has asked a million questions about you, but," she shrugged, "he's more my type."

Well, thought Adrienne, that took care of all the newcomers. But if Nolga didn't ask some other girl there would be a man too many.

Fortunately there was a rush and Nolga had to step back to stand waiting for the windows to clear, the foyer to empty.

"I've come for your share of the dinner money," Nolga whispered.

"But I'm not giving a dinner, Nolga."

"I meant to discuss it this morning."

Ah, thought Adrienne, that's why we were having waffles.

"But after the dreadful way you talked to me I

42

couldn't bring myself to tell you how these nice men longed to meet you and how I'd planned to bring a little fun into your life."

"I haven't stopped credit at the markets," Adrienne weakened enough to confess.

"The markets. My goodness, Addie, these are city men. I can't buy anything fit for them to eat any place in The Oaks."

Again Adrienne almost weakened; then she remembered Lakeville's dress shops. Let Nolga in her present mood reach there before her own letters cutting off credit did, and there'd be bills to pay.

"I should think you'd consider it a challenge to prepare a country dinner. I imagine the guests would enjoy it for a change. Besides, your Frank said something about a diet."

"He did?" She said no more. Collier, coming up to watch her patter out, laughed softly.

"You love that little nitwit, don't you, Addie?"

"I suppose I do," mused Adrienne. "She's rather like a kitten, always getting into mischief. Have you ever tried to discipline a kitten?"

Collier chuckled. "Seen their astonished look of pain at being slapped by the one they trusted most? Yes."

"And you feel cruel even while you know they must learn discipline."

"Addie, remember this: kittens grow up. Stop

giving in to Nolga's attempt to act younger than you. She isn't you know, except emotionally."

But it was one thing to know the truth, something totally different to act upon it.

"I wonder," mused Collier, "if half of Nolga's litle girl attitude isn't brought on by people treating her like a child. She might respond to being treated like an adult. Be an interesting experiment."

"All right," Adrienne said dryly, "I read you. I might add I've already started. I've cut off her credit."

The words were barely out of her mouth when one of the few persons in town who had the unlisted post office telephone number called.

"Addie, Mrs. Akars was just in. She said you wanted a delivery from Lakeville's Specialty House and wanted it charged here. The items," he read off a list, "weren't in character. How about it?"

"One last mad fling," groaned Adrienne. "You were right, Matt: I didn't give such an order. I was coming down this noon to change our account. From now on I'll pay cash for what I want. Anything Mrs. Akars wants is strictly between you."

It was a painful method of washing family linen in public, yet the merchants and many others at The Oaks knew of Nolga's extravagance. Perversely, they would respect both more for staying within their budgets.

"I'll try to catch her." Matt was sighing now. "She went into the ceramic shop. I think she's buying a new set of dishes. Andy was over a moment ago to see if Mame would part with the coffee server that goes with the set."

Adrienne knew the set: rusty red to match the fireplace, and deftly shaped. She had longed for it herself, but it had been beyond her means.

Cutting off her stepmother's credit seemed to be working in reverse.

"It might be smart to take an early lunch hour," Collier remarked, "and hide. The post office is not an arena for family rows, and something tells me there is one brewing."

"And where would one hide at The Oaks?" sighed Adrienne.

"Home would be the last place she'd look for you, wouldn't it?"

It would. And it would allow her time to do some necessary cleaning.

Adrienne sped down the lane, feeling the hounds of public opinion at her heels. Nolga was nothing if not vocal, and while the merchants would sympathize with her, there were townspeople who would sympathize with her stepmother.

If I could just shake some sense into her, she mused, hurrying to the kitchen door; make her see we can't go on like this.

She entered the room and stood defeated. The place was spotless, the dining ell a vision of potted plants, an aquarium and a cage of turquoise blue parakeets. From the living room came voices with a definite Swedish accent. Lars and Hilda of Lakeville, imported at five dollars an hour.

"There now," Hilda came in to beam at Adrienne "you give to us the money for this morning. We come back at five o'clock. We been here since eight. We finish early. Only eighteen dollars."

"But I didn't hire you Mrs. Peterson. I didn't even know you were here. You'll have to get your wages from the person who called you."

"From that one?"

Lars came in. "Miss Adrienne, you have the reputation of always paying. We put off good customers to come to you in emergency."

Adrienne nodded. Those two were always busy and worth every penny they charged became of their swift efficiency. If she did not pay them, goodness knew when Nolga would get around to it. It seemed unfair they should have to be the ones to suffer.

Yet what could she do? Take them into her confidence? Hardly that. And if Nolga were to find some means of paying them and continue this burst of entertaining, what then?

"I'm sorry," she said. "I think you know I've

not been able to hire outside help since my father died. Now if you'll excuse me—"

She turned back and hurried up the lane, looked up and down the street, then darted into the post office as into a haven. "You and your good advice," she muttered to Collier. "Now slip out and buy me a hamburger and coffee. I found the Akars place invaded—"

"With onions?" he asked, smirking. "And why did I suggest you go home?"

"It wasn't invaded with onions. I mean, why insult our patrons with every stamp sale? Just mustard or catsup or, if they're not fresh out, cyanide."

Nolga came in at noon, but so did half of Lakeville.

The fury with which she had entered died, gave way to incipient tears.

Adrienne felt if the post office could remain busy enough, Nolga might give up and go forth to do something on her own. It did, and Nolga did. But when she returned she wore triumph like a banner.

"Add—oh, excuse me, Mrs. Duvall. I just wanted to speak to Addie a minute. Add, sign this."

Adrienne continued weighing Mrs. Duvall's package. Nut and raisin cake for her daughter in the city, she knew.

"Add—"

"Nolga, this is a place of business; personal matters can wait."

"Well, this can't!" A slip was thrust at Adrienne. "It won't take a minute."

Adrienne studied the printed note. It came from the bank and required her co-signature to release one hundred dollars to Mrs. Nola Akars.

Tessie left, Collier returned from a business club luncheon looking thoughtful. "Add, I've been asked some curious questions today. Would you say there was something more than spring in the air?"

"Such as?"

"Seems these men who've come to town this week aren't sitting in the lobby, resting. They're up to something."

"But they didn't come together," she reasoned aloud. "Do you think they've ever met before?"

"As far as the hotel knows, they haven't. And they have each registered from widely different parts of the country. Why not keep your ears open tonight? They're all coming to your place for dinner, aren't they?"

"Not all," she replied thoughtfully. "Burrows isn't. But then, neither am I. I'm having dinner in town and on orders, slipping quietly to my room by the old side door so I won't be seen."

" 'He who refuses to pay the piper can't party,' " misquoted Collier. "The wife and I would be proud to have you."

Adrienne thanked him and said she had other plans. She had, but they were nebulous. Above all, she wanted privacy without fear of interruption in which to think, to plan.

Gratefully she watched evening close in. This hadn't been an easy day.

On Sunday she was going out with Rodman Burrows. Even his blunt admission he had had a purpose in asking her couldn't dim the glory of a date with a man, especially a man who interested her as much as Burrows.

Idle for the moment, she sat, staring out through the high stamp windows to the wall beyond, a wall plastered with photographs and descriptions of men wanted; faces she'd seen for so many months she no longer actually saw them.

A car drew up outside, headlights turned high, lighting up one panel of faces.

"That's queer," she whispered. "That one there, second from the end, I know I've seen him some place. Oh, but I couldn't have, not here in The Oaks."

The occupant of the car came in, came up to a window, smiling, "Mrs. Akars said you might call on some of Uncle Sam's minions to take over and let you off earlier. I'm here to take you home."

"Oh?" Adrienne made it a question. "It's too late for that."

"To take you home, or for the minions?" asked Craig Jones.

Wouldn't Nolga place her in such a position? thought Adrienne. I would be churlish to refuse, and what could be gained at this late hour?

"Too late to call anyone. There, the mail truck is just pulling in; I'll be another three quarters of an hour."

"Good; then I'll be back at that time." He hesitated a moment. "You know, Miss Akars, we're all of us going there to meet you. It seemed the only way, as you're such a recluse."

Chapter Five

Never had The Oaks post office received a more thorough end-of-the-day grooming. Pads and pens and pencils were aligned, wastebaskets emptied and dusted.

"If we hadn't a contract with Pussy-foot," observed the half amused, half annoyed Collier, "I could let you wash windows."

"I'm sorry," sighed Adrienne. "I just don't want to go home. I detest being manipulated this way. First I'm told I'm no longer wanted, then placed in a position where I literally have to appear."

"Forget yourself," suggested the postmaster, "and think of what you may learn if you keep your wits about you."

Adrienne stared at him a moment, brightened, then saluted. "Will you?"

Craig Jones was waiting. Adrienne was a little amused at the courtesy he showed, handing her into his car as though she were some precious but fragile fare.

Driving to the Akars', he spoke of The Oaks in glowing terms. The place had a great future. Look at the lake frontage, which only needed development. And the railroad spur—how wise the city fathers were to see the franchise was kept up. The old depot had been on the Akars place, hadn't it?

The topics were safe, but Adrienne was wary of questions. She had had one bad experience early in her post office days. A man seeking a divorce had sent an investigator who had asked innocent civic questions, then, when she was off guard, had thrust in a pertinent one in an innocent tone. Her father had acted as though she'd committed treason in time of war.

Yet Burrows intended to ask her questions; why did she feel so safe about her date with him? She supposed because he'd blatantly admitted his intentions.

The Akars house loomed against the last of the afterglow, budding trees towering around it. Inside, it looked equally beautiful, and Adrienne felt as though she were seeing it for the first time in years.

The kitchen seemed milling with people. Nolga had invited Dotty Doughterty, a young widow from Lakeville, a perfect foil with her sharp brunette vivacity. At the moment she seemed to be concentrating upon Van de Mark.

Smith was calmly performing some rite at the stove, a towel tied around his waist.

Why, I like him, Adrienne thought, surprised, after their introduction. What Nolga had called stuffiness, Adrienne believed was no more than natural reserve.

But she did not care for Frank Van de Mark. His sudden abandonment of Dotty when she came in, his bland assurance that she, Adrienne, would find him by far the most attractive man of the three, offended her.

"Girl, you're better-looking every time I see you," he greeted her, "even after a hard day. Late, huh? One thing about Uncle Sam, folks think they can take advantage of him. Come in at all hours for their mail, want stamps, that sort of thing."

Adrienne gave him her nicest smile. "Or perhaps those of us working directly for him feel enough loyalty not to leap when the whistle blows."

At the moment she saw a surprised look in the eyes of Dan Smith. It was approving and also expressed a certain resignation. Now what had caused that?

Nolga rushed in with a suggestion Adrienne freshen up; dinner was about ready.

"I've told them," Nolga came up breathlessly once she was in her room, "that the woman who usually helps us became suddenly ill. Don't you dare let me down."

"Why did you risk having me present?"

"Because," she said, then looked puzzled, "for some reason every single one of them wanted you."

She waited a moment, then said, "I'm going to have Gypsy style my hair. Honestly, the change it's made in you." And she was away, back to her guests.

Adrienne shrugged. She might as well dress up to her hair. She had an old brick red and white print which had seen much better days, but the colors would complement the setting of the dining ell, and with costume jewelry it would look quite festive.

She changed quickly, then looked at herself in amazement. Goodness, she was almost beautiful. Brightened by the thought, she hurried downstairs.

Perhaps she could have slipped in unnoticed, but Nolga chanced to be looking her way and cried, "You've kept us waiting until everything is ruined. You needn't have changed."

This time Smith's dark eyes were brimming with laughter. "Still a few minutes to go on this," he said, and stirred masterfully.

It proved a delightful dinner party.

The old Akars house too seemed to rouse from its apathy, wearing its potted plants like a lei; speaking cheerily through the parakeets that finally had to be covered to achieve silence. Even the hearth fire danced more merrily.

"A charming place," observed Craig Jones. "It would be a pity to have it destroyed to make room for some modern atrocity."

"That from you?" jeered Frank. "I thought you were a land broker. What else do you raise besides atrocities?"

"We should keep this as a manor house," began Craig dreamily.

"Who knows whether manor houses will be in style seven years from now?" said Dotty spitefully.

Adrienne let the talk wash over her, listening intently without appearing to, evading direct answers to questions.

"It would always be a good industrial site." Adrienne snapped to attention as Craig's voice arose sharply in argument with Frank.

"Way out here? You crazy?"

"Maybe Lakeville will have grown this far by the time it's available," offered Dotty, "though Lakeville really has no industry."

"Neither does it have a railroad spur. And believe it or not, there are still industries that use rails for dispersement."

"Well, my goodness," cried Dotty," couldn't one be run in?"

"Little matter of franchise," murmured Smith. "And if you'll look at that lake bed, you'd know what it would cost to maintain it. As the Oaks already has the spur connecting on east with a main line—"

"For my money," Frank spoke again, "I'd size this up as another Carmel; place where artists and writers hang out. It's sure quiet enough, and has the lake, mountains, things they say they have to have for inspiration."

"We have a writer," Nolga agreed. "I've told you about him, Frank. You can meet him when the Weavers return from the south. They give lovely parties; such interesting people—"

"People from around here?" he asked doubtingly.

"Oh, no, house guests whom people from around here are invited to meet."

"All I have to say is that one writer and one artist like this Clive fellow don't make a colony."

"And that is all you have, one each?" Dan Smith was asking the question and asking it of Adrienne.

"I believe we have a few poets," she said quickly. "Whether they've published or not I don't know. But I doubt it, or I would; we all would."

"My goodness, yes," cried Nolga. "We've one old crone who stops everybody on the corner to chant her dirges. We all run, and the chant comes after us."

"I expect people in the post office like you," offered Frank, "know just about everybody's business. I mean, you'd see manuscripts going out, coming back, letters and maybe checks?"

"One summer," Adrienne answered thoughtfully, "Dad let me work in the Lakeville cannery. I stood at a belt watching the cans go by. A post office isn't too different except it is letters that go by. There are so many there isn't time to observe or care about any one of them."

She looked up to find Dan's eyes crinkled. Nolga also noticed and, weary of attention being concentrated upon Adrienne, said a little sharply "If any of you ever have the bright idea of getting post office information out of Adrienne, give up. Even I can't make her gossip about her job. Not that I ever really tried."

Frank said stiffly he was sorry Nolga had thought he was prying. He hadn't meant it that way; he'd only tried to find something Miss Adrienne might find of interest.

It was Dotty who suggested they go the Lakeville Drive-in Theater. Adrienne grasped the opportunity to slip out of the limelight. "With six, it would take two cars for comfortable riding. You run on; I'll clear the dishes away."

"I'll stay and help," Frank offered quickly.

"Thank you, no." Adrienne was equally quick. "That would make me feel I was spoiling the party."

After they had left she stood for a moment holding a tray, gazing down at the embers on the hearth. A peculiar evening, and what had she learned? Actually, nothing.

Craig Jones seemed fairly obvious. He was interested in promoting the sale of large tracts of land.

Frank Van de Mark was supposedly at The Oaks for his health. If his appetite was an indication of his physical condition, there was nothing wrong with his health.

He simply doesn't ring true, Adrienne mused.

She thought then of his interest in "artists and writers." Memory clicked back and brought up their first conversation, his interest in people who came late or early for their mail. Then, dovetailing in, came the sardonic words of the writer from the hills, Hobart Hanson. "I've some cousins who'd like to locate me. Prime moochers. Minute I earned a little money they moved in."

Adrienne gave a sharp nod. This could be one of them. She didn't now why, but the two men were of a type, belonged to each other somehow. Frank Van de Mark would be the kind who'd move in.

She allowed herself a mild query as to his normal business, what if anything he did for a living, then passed on to Dan Smith.

Of the trio she liked him the best, yet there was something secretive about him. He talked freely about where he was from and his business. An insurance adjustor on vacation, he said he was scouting out a site for a hunting club to which he belonged. They'd like to buy and have shelter up before next fall.

A tap at the door broke her reverie. For a moment she hesitated, then switched on the rear yard light to see the man of whom she'd been thinking standing there.

"Thought I'd give you a hand with the dishes," he greeted her. "I claimed to be the odd man and had the others drop me at the inn."

"Married?" Adrienne asked lightly.

"Call it a K.P. fixation."

"Nu-uh, you're Navy."

He gave her a quick searching look. "What else do you know about me?"

"Nothing, except," she smiled at him, "that your yen for helping with dishes was secondary."

She should not have said that. Now she had lost any chance of learning more about Smith. He'd drawn some invisible veil about him.

"You underestimate your charm, Miss Adrienne. Besides, I insist. You've worked all day. We have left quite a mess in the kitchen."

He worked with quiet efficiency and in a short time they were through. Out of courtesy she suggested coffee before the fire. Not that she was unwilling. She liked this man despite his extreme reserve.

"Tell me about your hunting club," she suggested as they sat watching flames wrap around small logs before bursting up the chimney.

"I can't without asking questions," he returned ruefully, "and you close up the minute one's posed. Habit, I suppose."

She nodded. "Most people want to ask about

post office business. I've found it easier to answer nothing than to be surprised into saying the wrong thing."

"Can you give me an instance of that?"

"I might give one of my father's; it happened long ago. A Lakeville man disappeared. His mother lived here. Apparently the wife and the man's mother were friends. Actually, the wife was watching the mother, hoping to find the absent husband.

"One day after the mother had mailed some letters, the wife rushed in and said to Dad, "Mother is worried about the address on that last letter; if you'll give it to me I'll dash out and check with her. I know you can't return the letter itself.' "

"A perfectly normal request," Smith agreed. "I suppose there are people who wonder what they've written after the letter is through the slot. And I assume the woman hoped to get the address in this way. What did your father do?"

"Told her to bring her mother-in-law in and he would show her her own letter. That stopped it."

Smith leaned forward to stir the fire, and Adrienne watched the ruddy reflection on his face, a thoughtful, withdrawn face, telling nothing. A challenge, she thought, and wondered what one might do to tear away that veil of reserve.

"I'm not interested in post office business," he said. "I'm thinking of you as an Oaks native. Most of the people I've met have moved in here within the last fifteen years and have been too busy to scout out the mountain districts.

"I thought perhaps your father, on fishing or hunting trips, had stumbled upon some paradise, a Shangri-la with a mountain meadow, an ideal building site, or even some old dwelling that could be converted."

"Except that Father was not a sportsman. His post office, his garden and rearing a small daughter took up his full time."

She waited a moment, then laughed a little." It sounds silly, but it's true. The hunters here prefer to go east of the mountains to new territory for elk, or on into Canada for moose. But then I imagine men hunt to get away from the familiar, don't they?"

He smiled and stood up. "Next time let's have a date with no questions asked. How about Sunday?"

Adrienne glowed a little as she answered. Imagine already having a date. Life had changed with this influx of men.

"Then I'll try again. I'll be around for a while, off and on. Have to wait for the north to be cleared before I can scout up there. Realtors here tell me that might be another two months. Maybe I can drum up some business."

"Adjusting?" asked Adrienne, and wished she'd watch herself. Why let the man find out she knew he was lying about something?

He left, and she went upstairs, puzzled.

Nolga was up and had breakfast ready when Adrienne came down the next morning.

"I'm not going to be embarrassed by you having breakfast in town," she began, "especially after last night. You have no idea what I went through yesterday."

"What or how much?" Adrienne quipped.

"You have to lend me money for the Petersons. You weren't fair at all. You clamped down so quickly I hadn't time to adjust, and with an emergency dinner—"

"After I'd paid your last month's bills, I had no money left, Nolga; barely enough to see me through the rest of this month."

"Yet you went to Gypsy."

"She'll wait. She knows me. Nolga, I couldn't go through another winter like last one."

"*You* couldn't!" Nolga lifted a ravaged face. "But you belong here. I don't. That's why I'm so desperate. Adrienne, I intend to marry one of these men if only to get away from here. I'm not smart and efficient like you are. I'm just not brave enough to start out in a strange place looking for work."

Adrienne leaned down to drop a kiss and drop a bit of advice. "I have to hurry, Nolga. And, darlin', listen. It doesn't take money to marry a man; not with your talent for making people want to take care of you."

Collier was interested in Adrienne's run-down of the previous evening, but she confessed she had nothing to report. "I am even more confused. I'm almost ready to believe each man is what he says he is."

It was a dull day at the post office and a dull day outside.

With surprise she saw the Akars car drive up as she was closing the windows. Nolga, vibrant with excitement, jumped out and ran in. "Wait," she cried. "Oh, Addie, the most wonderful thing has happened. I've been with Craig. We've gone all over the place. He's ready to buy our land for—just imagine—thirty-two thousand dollars."

Chapter Six

Adrienne computed mentally and arrived at the magnificent price of two hundred an acre. Then she wondered how Nolga could have forgotten they couldn't sell.

"I'll be out in a minute," she murmured. "Wait for me in the car."

She needed that minute or more to adjust. If the land was worth two hundred an acre, it was worth more. Purchase of the hundred and sixty acres meant development on a large scale, and Craig didn't appear to be the type of man to put up shacks.

Above all, how did Craig hope to get around the restraining clause in the will, or hadn't Nolga told him?

That was the first question Adrienne asked when she joined Nolga in the car.

"Oh, that." She snapped her fingers. "Craig says there's always an out. When we tried before there was no prospect of selling. With a bona fide offer, cash in escrow, we can plead hardship or something. Craig says wills were made to be broken. All we need is agreement between the two of us, you and I. You will agree, won't you, Addie?"

"Where are you going?" Adrienne asked as Nolga started to drive away from the post office.

"Craig's taking us to dinner in Lakeville so we can talk things over without people listening in."

"But I have a fitting at Gypsy's."

"You think that more important than this? Addie, this is an out. We can get away, start living."

"Now wait. Your share would be sixteen thousand, right? How much did we pay the Lakeville attorney to try to break the will before? We'd have to pay other attorneys. If we came out with ten to twelve thousand apiece, we'd do well. And how long would that last?"

"Honestly," Nolga slammed the car into a curb and jammed brakes so they both bounced, "of all the wet blankets! Addie, you never had a positive thought in your whole life."

"Could be I've been too busy paying for yours. But look, honey. Suppose we started a legal fight to break the will and couldn't. We'd still have to pay the costs. Have you the money to do that?

"Why not think we could?"

"Because the last time I thought that it cost me my savings. This time let's take it slow. We don't have to leap into this. If Craig really wants the land, a few more days won't matter to him."

She told Craig as much when a sullen Nolga had driven her to the inn.

"Oh, but now look," he protested. "This needn't cost you anything. We have a fine staff of attorneys on retainer; they'll look into things without you becoming involved at all."

Adrienne nodded. "A few more days won't matter, will they? I have time off due me. I'll take it next week and we'll go into it thoroughly."

She was watching as she spoke and saw an expression of dismay and of doubt, quickly covered by an affable, "How about Sunday?"

She shook her head. "Sorry; I've a date for Sunday. Make it Monday." And then, as Nolga was to go in Craig's car, she slid into the driver's seat of the Akars car for the first time in weeks and drove off.

The Oaks Drive-In was not open for outside service, but Adrienne obtained a box dinner, then drove to a lonely spot on the lake.

When she was through she drove to Gypsy's and asked if she might put in a call to Lakeville. "And, Clive, I'd like you to listen in. I'm going to need someone to talk to."

Her call completed, she spoke to old Judge Cobb. "May I retain you by telephone, Judge? I may be needing some legal advice. Meanwhile, is there any way to learn if anyone has appeared at the County Hall of Records to check on the Akars will contest?"

"If you are free to talk, can you tell me why you want to know?"

She briefed him on Craig Jones' offer, especially on his assurance the will could be broken.

"I'll find out first thing in the morning and let you know. As for breaking the will, I doubt it. Remember, I drew it up. Your father was afraid of undue influence being brought to bear on Mrs. Akars and you suffering as a consequence."

That seemed to take care of that, Adrienne thought as she turned to Clive and Gypsy and told them of the offer.

"Wonder what's up," Clive mused. "Something in the air besides spring. That offer points up something. Yet as you say, if it's bona fide it should be a lot higher."

"Couldn't it be an initial offer?" Gypsy asked.

"Yes, a trial run. But it's more than that. Why a big housing project here? Neither The Oaks nor Lakeville has the payroll potentials to bring in."

"Oh, well, maybe Jones has some grandiose scheme to turn The Oaks into a retirement center."

"In this climate?" Clive jeered.

Gypsy held her hand out to Adrienne. "Come on; let's get beautiful."

"Wait a minute," urged Clive. "Thinking about what I said. If Jones needs your signature now before the preliminaries, that means he's afraid someone else is in the market."

"So I play for time," agreed Adrienne, and

laughed. "Imagine anyone wanting that barren stretch, let alone two promoters."

Two promoters. Frank? Dan? Or could it be Burrows? Frank had never stated his business. Dan had said he was an insurance adjustor. And of course Burrows had said he was an engineer. Frank then was the only one unidentified, yet Adrienne couldn't imagine him representing any company of any size.

In the studio, while Gypsy cut a soft kelly green to her figure, Adrienne talked freely. "I'd have been in over my ears had you not let me see what I was doing to Nolga."

"Do you think she has learned anything from it?"

"Only learned not to expect me to pay. I doubt if she understands, and goodness knows she doesn't believe it is for her own good."

"And how have you felt? Any better?"

"Well, three men asked me for a Sunday date," Adrienne laughed. "But there was a joker. Each one admitted it wasn't my fatal charm. The one I accepted came right out and said he wanted to question me."

"Honest if not diplomatic. Want to tell me which invitation you accepted?"

"Burrows.' "

"Oh?" Gypsy spit pins out into her hand. "I met him at the Lakeville Bank. Believe it or not, J.C. was fawning on him. I liked him. Girl, here's where I get busy. If you're going out with him, this dress must break the ice. And you need a hat. I think I've some ribbon to match. And a bag and shoes. Have you some to contrast, or can you borrow Nolga's?"

Adrienne shook her head and remembered she wanted a lock for her wardrobe door. It would be easier than quarreling with Nolga after she'd taken—and shortened—such a frock as this.

They talked then of the new men in town, Gypsy laughing with Adrienne at the idea of Frank Van de Mark being a private eye.

"He seemed interested in artists and writers last night," Adrienne said. "Oh, and while we're on that subject, what type of man writes crime stories?"

"Mysteries or factual? The latter I'd say are written mostly by newsmen covering courts and criminal beats. Not thinking of taking it up, are you?" she teased. "But seriously, Adrienne, if you intend to stay on at The Oaks, you should have an avocation. Our winters are so long."

"Gardening would be my hobby in a climate like this. No, I think I'll sit out this summer and see what happens."

They went over some frocks Adrienne had sent up earlier. Nondescript affairs she'd thought them, but Gypsy's deft touch had transformed them.

"Here, this gray is finished. Treat yourself to a coral sweater and earrings. Oh, and here's the right shade rouge and lipstick. Once you start living right you can forget the rouge. Now you need it for sparkle."

Sparkle. Gypsy added that to each garment, while Adrienne marveled. Gypsy, with a Lakeville shop of her own where she commanded the highest prices in that area, seemed perfectly willing to meet Adrienne's immediate need by refurbishing her old bargain rack frocks.

"I shouldn't let you do this," Adrienne said. "I'll admit it's fun to think of line and color and accessories again, but where will I have a chance to wear these?"

"Wear them and the chance will come. You'll attract it. Not because of the frocks, Addie, but because you'll light up inside.

"The best designer in the world can't turn a drab, unhappy woman into a beauty. It's the inner sparkle that does it. And now I'll get down off my soapbox."

Adrienne had sparkle the next morning. Nolga showed her displeasure by remaining in bed. Her stepdaughter happily telephoned a friend in The Oaks' only department store, and within an hour of her arrival at the post office the coral sweater and earrings were delivered.

By then they were of secondary interest. Mail was beginning to arrive for Jones, Van de Mark and Burrows.

Adrienne sorted the batch containing letters for

the first two. A long business letter with a Belmont Land Company return address for Jones, and a dainty scented letter in feminine handwriting with only the address.

Not his wife, Adrienne reasoned. Wives rarely bother with perfume.

Of course he'd told them he'd been widowed four years ago, but one couldn't be sure.

Two letters for Van De Mark. A cheap envelope with Frank's name and address written in a cramped hand and no return address. From his mother, Adrienne thought, and noted the postmark, which didn't necessarily mean he came from the same town or state.

The second letter she held a moment as though to gain something from it by osmosis, then slipped it into the box thoughtfully.

Collier came up, looking wise. "Beginning to see the light," he commented, and Adrienne glanced at the sheaf of letters he had ready for Burrows' business box.

"Are you sure he and Jones aren't working together?"

"Quite sure," she murmured. "He said he was anxious to meet Burrows."

Half an hour later Burrows came in, gave her a quick, admiring look, said, "Be back in a few minutes," and went out to the car with his mail.

The moment the morning rush was over he was back.

"Now about the time and place of meeting—" he began. "I've found a riverside cafe over by Junction City I thought you might enjoy. At what time shall I call for you?"

"Will you consider me devious if I suggest you do not call at my home for me? Something tells me we'd have a hard time getting away."

Adrienne wondered if she heard a small sigh of relief as Burrows said, "then you choose the place."

She thought of Lovenia Cantrell in Lakeville. Lovey had told her she was always welcome to spend the night at her place.

"Can you wait a moment?"

She called the Lakeville Library, told Lovenia her problem and was greeted with, "My dear, I understand, and you're more than welcome. Come early and have dinner with me."

Burrows, purportedly reading his mail, caught her message and went on. Adrienne, at the stamp window, looked across the street to where Frank Van De Mark was busily investigating the contents of a notion store window display. It provided an excellent reflection of the post office.

"You would choose a time like this for a vacation," grumbled Collier. "Now I'll have to wait a week to find out what you learn Sunday."

"You, in your position, wait a week?" she chided. "You've already found out more than I know."

He nodded solemnly. "Just happened to notice

72

which letter Burrows opened first, and I had it made; everything fell into place. You know, Addie, this job can be an awful strain on a man or woman. I don't even dare talk to the wife. She might let something slip over the bridge table."

Judge Cobb didn't call until noon. He reported he'd had Stanton junior run him down to the county seat so he could investigate without causing comment.

"Two parties signed in to view the Akars will contest records, Addie. I checked and found both lawyers. The first is on the staff of the Ewa Electronics Company; the second is a legal representative of the Belmont Land Company. Addie, are you there?"

"Yes, Judge. That buzz you heard was my brain."

"Both men would know there could be no further contest. I'm going to investigate further. Can you come to the office Monday at about two o'clock?"

"Yes," she agreed in a thoughtful voice. "Maybe then I'll have something to contribute."

"Meanwhile don't you sign anything, anything at all, understand?"

"Don't worry."

"And tell your addle-pated stepmother—"

"Oh, my goodness," breathed Adrienne. "How can I keep her from it, if she hasn't signed already? Judge, I have no control over her at all."

"She can dispose of nothing," he comforted her, "but she might tie herself and you into a knot it would be costly to untie. But I don't think this is the time to talk to her. We'll have to risk it."

When she didn't comment he asked sharply, "Addie, are there any strange men at The Oaks?"

"Oh, my, yes. I can place three of them, but there's one man too many."

"Well, stay away from them."

"No sir," replied Adrienne. But the Judge, convinced she'd automatically given assent, had hung up.

Nolga came in just before noon. "Addie, the car is down the street with a flat and the garage won't give me credit. You just have to do something. Where did you get that gorgeous sweater? Here I am having to walk, and you buy things like that. Oh, let me wear it this afternoon."

When she paused for breath Adrienne was ready. "I'll do something, but I must have the use of the car. Between Craig and Frank and Dan you needn't walk."

"Dan never invites me anywhere; he's interested in you, Addie. About the sweater—"

"No. I'll call the garage and have them fix the tire."

"I'm afraid you'll have to buy a new one. Oh, and I'm about out of gas."

The car was also nearly out of oil. But the exterior was polished, and there were new seat covers.

Adrienne left the car at the garage for the afternoon; the boys were sworn to turn it over to no one but herself.

Gypsy was right about one thing. If one wanted something strongly enough to stand up and fight for it, it usually dropped into one's lap.

Chapter Seven

Adrienne found the Duncan house alive with lights and laughter.

"What's going on, Gypsy? Are you having a party, and am I intruding?"

"Better than that, you are the guest of honor. Nolga called. She wanted you home for dinner and the evening, and I told her you planned to be here until late; a crowd of my friends were coming in to meet you."

"They were?"

"They are now. You didn't want a conference with Jones before next week, did you?" Gypsy asked anxiously. "And I know you're going to Lovey's tomorrow."

"Thank goodness for both of you. I was planning to go on to a movie."

Adrienne drove home slightly bewildered. She'd had a delightful evening. Gypsy's friends were older than she but interesting: the Rock Goodmans (Adrienne remembered when Matilda had been the Lady Mayor of Lakeville and the trouble she'd had); Nance Elliot, the woman's editor of the *Courier;* and the Jim Elliots, owners and publishers of the paper.

There were a few others, all interested in the political and business welfare of the area.

As Adrienne had anticipated, she was home and asleep before Nolga came in. Nolga awakened her in the morning to sit at the foot of the bed wearing a determined expression and a negligee.

"Craig thinks you don't like him," she charged. "You go out with everyone else and avoid him."

Adrienne sat up and yawned happily. Begrudgingly Nolga said, "You're even pretty at this time of a day. I'd like to know what Gypsy's done to you."

"You're shivering; can't we finish this downstairs?"

"Not until you tell me why you dislike Craig."

"But I don't. You said it. I didn't, and I doubt if Craig did. He just happened to arrive when the worm turned over. Right now the worm is busy turning into a butterfly. I'll see him next week. Now do go down to the fire or wrap up in a blanket."

"Aren't you even going to tell me about last night? Was Dan Smith there or that other man, Burrows?"

"Just Lakeville people." No, they hadn't discussed the Akars property or the new men in town or asked post office questions.

Nolga was mollified but Adrienne wasn't. She wanted to warn Nolga about signing any papers unless an attorney was present, but feared if she did Jones might try to jump the gun and gain at least the one signature.

Dotty would be spending the night with her. And Adrienne didn't care for her, Dotty was shrewd enough to advise Nolga and bold enough to do it in public.

When she drove off after the Saturday noon closing, the car seemed to be bouncing with joy, or was it her own high spirits?

Just a week ago she had dragged herself unhappily home through a chill rain with nothing but a lonely weekend ahead. Today she would lunch in Lakeville with a former high school friend, shop around town, go to Gypsy's salon to pick up frock and hat, then spend the night with Lovenia, always a treat.

And tomorrow!

Tomorrows did come. Adrienne stood twirling before a full length mirror. "Do I look all right?" she asked Mrs. Cantrell.

"Yes, Adrienne, you do. You've always looked all right, but like a lamp that wasn't lighted. Now this young man—"

"He's only a last straw, Lovey, about as romantic as a slide rule, but I owe him a debt of gratitude. He made me see myself as I'd become."

"Well, here he is. My goodness," she peered out of the window, "if I were forty years younger—"

Lovenia Cantrell beamed on them both as they walked to the car.

"Your sister?" Burrows asked.

"New clothes," Adrienne answered.

"Couldn't be; I never notice clothes. You haven't lost your heart to one of those—"

"Heart? No, it was my temper I lost, or perhaps my patience with myself. I quit being noble."

A slide rule, she decided, had a sense of humor, and Burrows' was contagious. The squared lines broke into angles, and his eyes became sherry-colored instead of grey.

"Guess everyone goes through a period of that," he confided, putting the car into traffic. "I did. It nearly wrecked the family and the business. I retrenched at the wrong time, and our competitors thought our finances had hit the skids. Mother arranged a physical check-up, but Dad used a verbal belaying pin.

"Dad said rugs were made to be walked on. If I wanted to be a rug, I should get out of the construction business."

"A friend, Gypsy Duncan, said when self-sacrifice becomes self-pity, it is the worst form of egotism."

He eased the car onto a turn-off that gave a spectacular view of the valley below and the coast range. "I almost broke today's engagement. Now wait. It was not because I didn't want to carry through, but because I wanted to make another of a different type."

Adrienne, whose breath had caught, released it slowly.

"Would you mind rerunning that slowly?" she asked.

This time the squared features softened and a rueful light touched Burrows' eyes. "My initial reason for asking you changed. I learned what my company needed to know. That meant a much more important question to ask. It seemed only fair that I should ask that with your attorney present. You do have a legal advisor, don't you?"

"Yes," she almost whispered the admission. "And why didn't you?"

"For two reasons. Time has become important, for one. The other," and now he looked at her seriously, "I didn't want to wait. I wanted to know you, and I'm not saying that to gain favor. You believe that, don't you?"

"I'd like to."

"All right. I'll prove it. We'll go on, have a leisurely dinner and drive home, and I won't mention business at all. How's that?"

Adrienne looked down on a valley polka-dotted with pale yellow green foliage, looked up at a sky polka-dotted with small white clouds, then looked at Rodman Burrows.

"Where did you learn so much about women?" she demanded.

"About women? Oh, but I never have. I have two handsome brothers who work in town. I'm the one they send shuttling back and forth across country. I never have time to meet any. Oh-oh," He broke off, then tipped back his head and laughed.

"Exactly," she agreed dryly. "I'd be so thoroughly miserable wondering about business I wouldn't enjoy anything at all. You couldn't talk now and then let us forget it or not as we choose?"

"Why not?" He eased the car to a better position, one that gave view of the great bulk of a snow-covered mountain at the north end of the valley, set the brakes and turned to her. "I'll have to begin by telling you our business." Then he caught a flicker in her dark eyes and shook his head. "I have been stupid, haven't I? You'd know from incoming mail. But say, you don't—"

"We don't," she assured him. "We don't even tell our families what we chance to see. They might not be aware of its importance and talk to the wrong people."

He gave a bit of his background then. His father had been a construction engineer and he had followed him in his business, but his two older brothers had gone in for electronics. Now the senior Burrows and himself built the plants that would house the work of his brothers.

The plants were pin-pointed at salient spots where their products could be dispersed with the least possible handling. By choice they sought places such as The Oaks so they might draw on local people as employees.

"We've found stable home-owning men and women are the best security risks," he explained.

"However," and this he admitted ruefully, "we have also found there is a leak in our organization some place. The moment we choose a locality, promoters sweep in to buy up the land, some to build and sell, some merely to hold for the inevitable higher prices a new plant brings in its wake."

Adrienne shifted uncomfortably. Jones, Smith and Van de Mark? And only one of the three had admitted he dealt in land.

"Do they sometimes gain an option on land you want?" she asked.

"Not necessarily, though we would prefer buying direct from the original owners. We let them know the value of the land to us. The promoter doesn't."

Adrienne nodded. Jones had offered thirty-two thousand for the one hundred and sixty acres, and she had questioned his offer.

Burrows went on to say the scout they had sent out to this area, detailed to The Oaks because of the railroad spur, had found the Akars property ideal for their needs. It had everything they wanted, including an artesian well that promised an unlimited water supply.

The next investigator checked with the railroad

company; then Burrows had been sent out to begin negotiations.

"Our first man asked no direct questions about the land. We did know it was part of an estate inherited by a wife and a daughter. As it was nonproductive, there was the assumption they would be interested in disposing of it.

"When I saw you at the post office that first day, I had just arrived in town. The Akars name was important to me, so when I came in the second time and learned your identity I wanted to meet you, talk to you—"

"Why not Mrs. Akars?" asked Adrienne.

He hesitated a moment. "She'd been pointed out to me. I'd seen her before. Each time she was in the company of a man I'd identified as working for a subsidiary of a land firm that always managed to buy before we'd completed our negotiations."

"And you've no idea how this company learns of your plans?"

"I have, but the others don't agree. I think it's a woman employee."

He glanced at his watch and remarked they'd better finish en route; he'd ordered dinner for one o'clock.

They drove for a little while in silence; then Adrienne picked up the story. "So you came to The Oaks, investigated and learned the Akars couldn't sell for another seven years. You heard of the will contest and had some lawyer representing you check the records of the will contest. Didn't he find that pretty conclusive?"

The car had wobbled a little as Burrows had looked at her in surprise. "Definitely conclusive. Yet we believed there was an out some place our man had missed. The land company doesn't waste time or expense money. Their man was continuing to see the widow and trying to reach the daughter, but with no success there."

"You spied?" Adrienne asked angrily.

"No, just played in luck. Fellow at the hotel—Van de something—has been keeping his eye on Mrs. Akars. He'd overheard a conversation between the three of you, this Jones, Mrs. Akars and yourself. You'd been definite about not discussing something with him until the following week.

"This Van chap came into the hotel laughing, told another man of the incident. I was an innocent bystander. I'd have cheered had I not felt like such a heel. I'd made a date with you to ask you questions."

"The difference," murmured Adrienne, "is that you told me your reason, allowed me to be on guard against giving out information I glean on the job. The others start an innocent conversation, then throw surprise questions, hoping to catch me off base."

"Have they succeeded?"

"No. I have an instinctive distrust of one; the other is too much of a gentleman."

"Or knows when he's whipped. So do I, and glory in it. Now the rest can wait until you arrange for me to meet your attorney."

Maybe the rest could, Adrienne thought, but she wasn't sure she could.

"I have an appointment with him tomorrow afternoon," she said, "if you would like to meet me there."

The little chalet which sat in a craggy canyon had never looked more enticing to Adrienne.

For a man who said he had had not much experience with girls, Burrows proved an excellent host. He'd reserved a corner window table looking down on the rushing stream and up the canyon to the mountain.

He seemed as pleased as she felt when she was recognized by the proprietor, and later, when guests from another table stopped by for a moment.

He waited until fresh brook trout, crisp in brown blankets, came in on a bed of fresh watercress, then said ruefully, "I don't suppose anything would now induce you to stay on, or don't you dislike The Oaks?"

"Of course I don't."

"I feel a little better. I was afraid if we found some way to take over your land, you'd fly out the moment the papers were signed. I'd like you to stay around. I intend to be here for some time; there are other tracts, you know. I'd try to see you weren't too bored."

Across the room Mrs. Hedspath, of The Oaks, said to Mr. Hedspath, "Jack, it's the strangest thing. I've always thought Addie Akars on the plain side, but today she's beautiful. That good-looking young man just said something that made her light up. I wonder who he is."

It was a perfect day, from lunch to the spectacular sunset. She was ready for the suggestion they go on to the county seat to a movie, have a bite afterwards, then drive back by the new road.

"You don't know how I've enjoyed this," she said as they pulled into Lovenia's driveway.

"You don't know how I have," he returned. "Sunday in a strange place can be ghastly. I've enjoyed every minute. See you tomorrow then?"

Adrienne wasn't sure she could live until the next day, but she did. She slipped her car quietly out of Lovenia's garage and, after the long drive around the foot of the lake, into her own. She was relieved to find the house dark.

Inside, she found a note propped on the kitchen sink. "Spending the night with Dotty. May return tomorrow and may not; we're planning a grand celebration. Call me there if you need me."

A grand celebration? Adrienne carried the note upstairs and stood a moment in the upper hall looking out on The Oaks. Now what was Nolga up to, or was she baiting her?

By morning her spirits had revived.

Cloudy weather gave her an excuse to wear the red car coat Gypsy had contrived out of an old one she'd almost thrown away. It was gay and relieved the severe black dress with its white collar she would have to wear until further street clothes were available.

Judge Cobb seemed delighted to see her, though he assured her nothing could be done to relieve the will situation.

When Burrows came he told him the same, though reluctantly.

"But, Judge Cobb," Burrows said, "suppose my company offered to lease the land for seven years at a good figure, could you give us an option to purchase at the end of that time?"

"Well, bless my soul," sputtered the old man, "it never occurred to me anyone would want it that bad."

Chapter Eight

If it hadn't occurred to the Judge, it certainly had never entered Adrienne's mind. Land was something upon which someone built, and to build required clear title.

"We don't need that much," Burrows was saying. "We do want the warehouse, the area along the spur track and plenty of room for expansion.

"Our attorney wondered if it would be possible to cut off the home property, leave it clearly in the possession of the heirs. If not, we will rent it back to them at a dollar a year."

"Adrienne," Judge Cobb's voice broke her absorption, "how do you feel about the old house?"

"I used to love it," she replied, hardly aware she was talking. "Maybe I saw it through Dad's eyes. Then after he married it was right that Nolga make changes, be able to feel it was her home, so I moved outside. She didn't like gardening. What?" She broke off, embarrassed. "Judge, what were you asking?"

"I believe you've answered. Now run along and buy yourself an ice cream soda. This young man and I want to talk man talk."

"As though I hadn't outgrown sodas," chided Adrienne.

"Come back in an hour."

A few moments later she found herself in the drugstore, sitting at the soda fountain, a tall foaming glass before her.

"Dick, I ordered coffee," she wailed.

"No, you didn't, Miss Addie. You said chocolate soda, didn't she, Emmy?"

She must need a vacation, Adrienne thought. Imagine being that addle-pated at the post office.

A car pulled into a vacated parking space as Adrienne waited for the hour to pass. Three persons got out: first Frank Van de Mark, then Dotty and finally Nolga, Frank literally lifting her from the car.

Adrienne held her breath, but they moved away, and she took advantage of their shopping in some nearby store to hurry to the Judge's office to finish out her wait in his reception room.

It wasn't long. Burrows came out, accompanied by Cobb, who nodded at Adrienne. "I'd suggest you two not go out together until after I have talked with Mrs. Akars."

"She's in town," Adrienne began.

"I don't doubt that. But this must wait until I've talked to Mr. Burrows' legal advisor and have everything ready to present to her. I'll get in touch with you, Burrows. Adrienne, come in."

Adrienne wafted in and sat down to have the

Judge suggest dryly that she come down out of the clouds.

"Now tell me," he barked, "how far is Mrs. Akars involved with this land company man, Jones?"

"Involved?" Adrienne toyed with the word. "I don't know that she is. I think she saw him as a means to an end. He was interested in our land. He made an offer even after his company attorneys had checked the will contest.

"I think, Judge, that this has been harder on Nolga than it has been on me. She's older. Waiting out seven more years means wrinkles and grey hair to her. Nolga is the type to marry again."

"Well, why doesn't she get out and get married? There's nothing in the will holding her to The Oaks."

Adrienne tried to explain that there were women who feared starting out without some money to see them through, especially when they had no real profession.

"She worked before she married your father," Cobb said truculently. "Trouble is, both he and you have spoiled her."

"I've stopped," Adrienne assured him.

"Now then," he drew a long sheet of legal cap toward him, "this is roughly the Ewa proposition. They will pay twenty-four thousand a year for the lease of your land, fifty percent of that to be charged off the ultimate purchase price."

90

That seemed more than fair. It meant that she and Nolga would have an extra eighty-four thousand between them during the seven-year wait, and whatever extra the Judge and the Ewa people would determine was the right price for the land.

There was little else he could tell her. "Just keep still about this until I've talked to Mrs. Akars."

"Tell me how," groaned Adrienne. I promised to talk to Jones this week. I've been putting him off."

"Wait; let me think. You're taking time off, aren't you? You're a pretty good driver. Fine; just a minute. Annie," he spoke into the intercom, "get my wife on the phone."

Within a few minutes Adrienne was speeding toward The Oaks, the car of young Stanton Cobb behind hers.

It took only a few moments to pack, less time than it took to write the note she would leave for Nolga.

"Dear," she wrote, "forgive me for running off this way. I was offered a marvelous trip to the city with Lakeville friends. Will be away a few days; do have Dotty over to visit you. I'll write from the city when to expect me. Such fun to be getting away from the grind."

It seemed a devious method of getting away from a conference with Jones, but, reasoned

Adrienne, even the best general avoided combat, if possible, until his reserves were brought up.

The judge was waiting for her at the Cobb home. "Here." He thrust a roll of bills at her. "I've the authority to advance you this. Have a good time. And, Adrienne, don't spend it on Mrs. Akars."

She spent only half of it on Nolga.

They reached the capital the first night, the city early enough the next day to do a little shopping. Then Mrs. Cobb told her to plan her own time; she had duty visits to relations who would call for her.

Adrienne spent most of her first day alone, observing and being observed.

At dinner that night Mrs. Cobb asked, "Adrienne, what happened today to make you so thoughtful?"

"It didn't happen today; it's been happening for months," she replied absently. "People, lonely people, live almost next door to each other without knowing how much they have in common."

"And because of your position you are not free to tell them."

Adrienne looked up. "To tell them," she repeated. "But there is nothing to keep me from bringing them together outside post office hours and letting them find out for themselves."

For a moment she toyed with the idea. She would have simple intimate suppers. She could invite Burrows, or Dan Smith. Right there she stopped. How could she plan anything simple when at any moment Nolga might come in with Dotty and Frank? How quickly those two could ruin such an atmosphere as she needed to create.

Burrows. Of course when the land was leased she would have enough income to rent an apartment or a cottage, if Nolga didn't do likewise immediately. If she did, then she, Adrienne, would stay on at the Akars house.

"Adrienne, for a moment I thought you'd reverted," Mrs. Cobb remarked.

"For a moment I did," Adrienne conceded. "Defeatism is a difficult disease to cure. I have to remember what Gypsy said: when you start slipping back into it, start running in the opposite direction. Tomorrow I start running, to a bookstore."

She tried to explain her theory, "You can't say, 'Miss Whosit, Mrs Whatsit reads books on the same subjects in which you are interested.' You can say, 'Miss Whosit, here's a book I think you may enjoy. May I have it back the first of the week? Mr. Whatsit would like to borrow it.' Then tell Whatsit Miss Whosit will be through with said book Monday. After that you let their joint interests take their course."

"Of course you will have to read each of the books," warned Mrs. Cobb.

"Oh, dear," murmured Adrienne, and felt herself going into orbit, becoming at the same time a transcendentallist, a science fiction fan and a philosopher. At least there would be no more lonely evenings.

Up to her elbows in books the next day, Adrienne wondered what, besides engineering, Burrows liked.

Fishing, hunting? No, that was Dan Smith's field. Travel?

Judge Cobb called late Thursday. He had an appointment with Mrs. Akars the next day. It would be safe for them to return Saturday. He'd had a series of conferences with an Ewa attorney; as far as they both were concerned, they needed only the agreement of the heirs.

"Oh, and, Mother, tell Adrienne Rod wants her to pick up any late book on northern travel, Alaska or Canada, preferably first person. I think he's getting ready for a hot summer here."

Adrienne shopped early and read the first book that night at the capital, as they'd decided to return in two days. She skimmed through a second and third by rising early.

It was Judge Cobb who drove her from Lakeville to The Oaks.

"Want to talk to Mrs. Akars," he explained, "and talk to you first."

When they were under way he said Nolga had been in. She'd received his plans and suggestions with only a modicum of interest.

"I was a little surprised, Adrienne. I pointed out she would be receiving more money over the period of years; that she would immediately receive twelve thousand. I thought she would jump at it."

"Nolga lives in the now," Adrienne told him. "Ewa offers six thousand now. Craig Jones quoted thirty-two thousand. I doubt if Nolga really cut that in two, giving me my half. She knows she couldn't go far on twelve thousand but could make a big splash with the thirty-two."

"You mean she would really take your half if you'd let her?"

"She wouldn't see it that way. She firmly believes she looks after me. She would include me in her plans, her basic scheme to catch rich husbands for both of us. Now wait before you blow up. Nolga can't help being what she is; she's merely true to her specie."

"Well, as for her specie—"

"Whoa, back up, Your Honor. Who grows orchids? And just who has a thoroughly stinking orchid he treasures because it is so rare? Do you blame that blossom?"

"If you mean she—"

"I don't. I mean she is decorative and thrives only in a hothouse atmosphere."

She should have known better. The Judge hadn't wasted his time in court. He was an expert at rebuttal.

"Good thinking," he intoned, "but seems to me all of these rare orchids I dote on grow wild in their native habitat. I think we'd better find her jungle and ship her back to it."

From the looks of the Akars house the orchid had shipped herself off.

"Looks like a hurricane breezed in," remarked the Judge.

"No," Adrienne objected, "she carried rain water with her. Those stacks of dishes have not been touched by a drop of it."

Bewildered, the Judge picked up a toy whistle that unfolded into a snake when blown through, knocked over a conical cap of gay colors, kicked at a pompom.

"The celebration," wailed Adrienne, flew up the stairs to Nolga's room.

There was no sign Nolga had ever lived in it. Even the bed was stripped down and neatly covered with a spread.

Adrienne skidded downstairs. "She's taken off, bag and baggage," she reported. "But she hasn't changed fundamentally. She took my new coral sweater."

"If you'll break that down—" he pleaded.

"I'm awfully afraid she's about to be married."

Judge Cobb sat down heavily." The saints be praised," he intoned. "Now are you sure?"

"No, except that she spoke of a celebration, and there's the way that awful Frank Van de Mark—"

Her voice trailed off. She was back in the post office holding a letter between her hands. What was there about that letter that had made her feel it had come from a wife? Why not a sister, a girl friend, a cousin or merely a friend?

In another moment she was calling Dotty.

"Certainly she's here," Dotty replied. "After your infantile behavior it wasn't safe for her to remain there alone with you. Her attorney will get in touch with you when he's ready."

Carefully Adrienne replaced the telephone and turned to the Judge, her eyes two great charcoal circles in an oval of white.

"Dotts says Nolga's attorney will get in touch with me when he's ready."

"Then she isn't married." Judge Cobb seemed deeply disappointed. "Wonder whom she's retained. Probably someone with the Belmont Land Company's interests at heart, or pocket.

"Well, can you sit it out?"

"What else? I'm wondering if Ewa will consider it worth-while."

Judge Cobb started pacing in one direction, Adrienne in the other. The judge stumbled over a long-legged rag doll and addressed to it language used in court on defamation testimony only. Adrienne came down on a piece of broken crockery and completed its demotion.

"Addie, that sweater you talked about—what did you mean?"

97

"She was reacting normally in basic things. It meant to me that she was acting under pressure. Somebody is—"

"Bringing undue influence. Now who? The Jones fellow from the Belmont Company?"

Adrienne considered this.

"It sounds ridiculous, but I can't quite see him doing anything unethical. I think he'd strain every scruple to its limit to gain a point for his company, yet—"

"Then who?"

Dan Smith she discounted, Nolga didn't see enough of him. And she had no valid reason for believing Frank Van de Mark would take such a stand. What could he gain, especially as he was here for his health and not representing one of the two companies involved?

"Adrienne," the Judge spoke heavily, "you are in a position to gain the knowledge I am going to need to handle this case to the best of your interests. Mail coming in to Jones as representative of the Belmont Company is going to be vitally important to us, especially mail coming from the courthouse and the title companies. It is possible Belmont is buying up all available land around here for one of two purposes: another company or to force Ewa to meet their price.

"Letters coming from a title company, from absentee land owners—"

Adrienne was staring at him in shocked fascination. The implication that she was in a position to open financial prison doors for herself and Nolga to help Rod Burrows and to check the others was frightening.

Chapter Nine

The Judge rumbled on. Adrienne thought of taking sick leave, of quitting and turning her post over to Tessie. And then she realized she couldn't. Unlike Nolga, she hadn't even "a pittance" coming from her father's insurance. She had to work and save until she had enough to get away, or until some disposition was made of the estate.

"Stop looking so horrified," snapped Judge Cobb. "I was outlining possibilities to show you the position in which you had been placed; the daily temptation to make use of your knowledge."

"I wouldn't. I couldn't," breathed Adrienne.

"Great heavenly day, girl, I know that. You Akars lean over backwards. That's why everyone trusts you implicitly, myself included. I wanted to point out the strain under which you'd be working, the temptation.

"There is this about such a situation. Bring it out in the open, look at all of the possibilities, and it loses its force. It's the niggling little day-to-day evasions that eat into the spirit.

"Now then, repack your bag and come home with me. I'll send the Larsens over to clean up this mess."

"Thank you, but no." Adrienne explained work was what she needed, somethng to do with her hands to pass the time.

"Then get someone in with you, some reliable person who won't talk. You may have visitors if you don't. No sense subjecting yourself to useless quarrels."

Adrienne didn't scan a list of people; she scanned the mail that came into The Oaks. In another moment she was dialing for the one boardinghouse in town and asking for Miss Johnson.

"Miss Johnson," she was a little breathless, "I have a great favor to ask. I'm spending the weekend alone here at my home. It is necessary for me to have someone here whom I can trust. Do you have any important engagements you can't break, or could you be my guest?"

There was a moment of silence, then a rush of words. "Important engagements, in this town? Oh, Miss Addie, if I had I'd break them. Now what shall I bring? Need any groceries? Oh, and have you a sewing machine?"

"An old pedal affair; better bring a can of oil. I'll check on groceries; we can go back to shop."

The Judge departed, mollified, and Adrienne without stopping to change, began stacking dishes in soapy water to soak, then attempted to clean up the trash left on the floor.

She had barely piled up the heap to be burned

when Caroline Johnson drove in, took one look and cried, "What on earth has been going on?"

"A party, I'd say." Adrienne laughed. "And don't think I invited you to help clean up. I'd hoped to clear it away before you reached here."

"But I'd love helping, and hadn't you better change? That's a beautiful dress."

She went up with Adrienne, taking the guest room next to her, and they talked back and forth, Adrienne explaining the dress had been made over for her by Gypsy.

"To match the new you," breathed Caroline. "Addie, what's happened to you? You look different, somehow."

Adrienne could tell her part of it. She could say three new men had come to the post office to rent boxes and buy stamps; that they had treated her as a piece of office equipment.

"I expected them to drop coins in my mouth, use my arm for a lever, and wait for stamps and change to pop out. And I resented it. I revolted."

Caroline nodded. "I revolted, too, but I couldn't afford Gypsy. I borrowed to finish college. This is my first year of teaching, and there just isn't enough money to go around. You know teacher's salaries."

Adrienne nodded. "Cheer up. Some day civic pride in having the most beautiful school building is going to crash. Citizens will learn the hard way it is what goes on in a building that educates their young, and money will be channeled to a teacher's pay to hold her."

After they had cleaned up, washed the dishes and made coffee, they sat before the fire talking. Adrienne told her the reason she needed someone with her over the weekend.

Gypsy telephoned as they were leaving for the market. The men in her life were going to the Lakeville Armory. Could Adrienne spend the evening with her? Or could she come down to the Akars house?

"Adrienne, why are you hesitating?" she asked.

Laughingly Adrienne replied, "I'd love having you, but asking you is like inviting a plumber to dinner just after the pipes have burst. Caroline Johnson and I are about to plunge into alterations."

Gypsy said she had a beef curry ready; all they would need would be rice "and trimmings." She'd meet them at the market. If she brought her own car she could stay as late as she wanted.

Driving back in Caroline's modest small car, with Gypsy following, Adrienne was aware this was the first time since high school days that cars had lined up in the Akars driveway. Later that evening two others cars started in, then turned away.

Someone with some knowledge of lay psychology had planned to find Adrienne angry, lonely and morose, an excellent time to bring her to their terms.

She was exhilarated by two phone calls.

Rod Burrows called first. He thanked her for the books, then said they were a fine choice but a poor substitute for her company. He'd be over to pay her for them the moment Judge Cobb lifted the ban. She must think of him the next day closed in a room at the inn, reading.

The second call came from Dan Smith with an invitation to dine with him the next day. He'd been scouting and had found a place some thirty miles east he thought she'd enjoy.

"It's called The Halfway House. Seems the old post used to stop overnight there before going over the Mountain to The Oaks."

Gypsy obligingly lifted her voice, and under its cover she could tell him about her guest. "Well, fine. I'd enjoy meeting her."

To Adrienne that meant his interest in her had nothing to do with the current Akars land deal, and as Caroline was delighted to break the monotony of The Oaks routine, she accepted.

While Gypsy and Caroline made a hurried trip to the drugstore and the Duncan house, Adrienne sat thinking of Nolga.

Gypsy and Caroline returned. Gypsy waved her wand (her scissors) over the little schoolteacher's head and brought her out a changed creature. A tint shampoo, discreet make-up; then Gypsy stood her before a panel mirror and walked away.

Caroline was still saying, "I can't believe it," when Adrienne drifted off to sleep.

Sunday was a day of sun and shadow. Dan Smith sent his car swiftly up the two-lane highway over the eastern hills as though eager to reach his destination.

"Tarryville," he explained to the still bemused Caroline, "so called because those who stopped there tarried, the road on the lake was so formidable. And beyond that was a treacherous stretch over the swamp lands. Don't you know it at all, Adrienne?"

"Only as a post office," she admitted ruefully. "I do remember, as a child, going through on the train. There was almost nothing there—buildings falling down, only a few people and a few corrals for beef being shipped out."

The beef were still being shipped out, but the fame that had rebuilt the town was by courtesy of Hollywood. A spectacular western had been filmed there, and later a few episodes of a television series, enough to give glamour and draw visitors from the nearest inland city, forty miles farther east.

Topping the range, they came into country still snow-spotted but barren. The town from a distance huddled at the foot of a plateau. But when they drew near they found the streets lined with cars, even a few horses at the hitching rails.

Looking on the scene, Adrienne wondered just how Dan Smith had come upon this. It wasn't hunting country. Of course he could have come to The Oaks from the east, yet if so, why was he receiving his mail at Lakeville to the west? And why not The Oaks, as he was living there?

Only one reason, in her opinion. Lakeville had a large post office and an equally large staff. Smith must be aware of the risk of postal employees on a small staff noticing his mail.

"My," breathed Caroline, "isn't this just like the real west?"

"You couldn't get much farther west," Adrienne observed.

Dan smiled. "She means the conception most people who've never been to the coast have of it."

He'd reserved a window table. Adrienne was placed facing it and naturally, just as a mother identifies her own child, so did she identify the small post office, its door open.

Food was served as it must have been in the early days. Platters and deep bowls were slapped on the table by waiters with long mustachios. The speciality of the house was barbecued beef and hashed brown potatoes. And each person served himself.

Adrienne had just slipped a serving of beef onto her plate when something made her look up. She looked down as quickly. Dan Smith was watching her.

Across the street, just coming from the post office, reading his mail, was Hobart Hanson; a Hanson she wouldn't have recognized had it not been for the fact he wore a cap; this time a brown denim with a bill.

Someone passing spoke to him and he saluted absently. That meant local people were accustomed to him and he to them.

Now just why was he receiving his regular mail here, yet slipping in and out of The Oaks post office in such a peculiar fashion, using a private box there? And what of that old lumber camp he was supposed to be living in back in the mountains? There wasn't a tree for miles.

"See someone you know?" asked Smith.

Chapter Ten

Adrienne looked up, startled.

"I hope not," she said, looking back at the beef. "I'm not a cannibal, and we don't run beef at The Oaks any more."

For her the day was spoiled. Smith hadn't invited her to dinner because he wanted her company. Somehow he had known about Hobart Hanson coming to the Tarryville post office on Sundays and had hoped she'd identify him as one who also came to The Oaks. Yet Dan Smith couldn't be one of Hanson's "mooching" cousins. He simply was not the type.

Caroline broke in with a laughing account of a baby chick she'd been given as a child; told how they'd raised the Easter gift until it became a nuisance and was destined for the pot, only none of the family could eat it.

As she talked she watched the glow fade from Addrienne.

"You're not enjoying this," Smith accused her.

"Sorry, a bit of a headache," she apologized.

"She's had enough this weekend to make her ache all over," Caroline declared loyally.

"So I understand. One reason I thought getting away from The Oaks might break the tension."

Adrienne really looked at him then. His eyes showed only a tender concern for her welfare. She was certainly growing fanciful. Simply because he'd asked a normal question she had jumped to the conclusion he'd brought her there for a purpose. And wasn't she the girl who scolded Nolga for jumping to conclusions?

Smith sent the waiter for aspirin, and Adrienne had to take it. Then, subdued but happier, she finished and approved the menu, right to the end of a deep dish apple pie.

By the time they drove home some of the glow had returned, and Caroline's spirits lifted even to the point of suggesting they stop at the hump to watch sunset turn The Oaks into a toy town of painted blocks.

"Are you staying with Miss Akars long?" Smith asked as they drove in the lane.

"As long as she'll put up with me," Caroline replied.

"Good. Adrienne," he turned to her as he parked, "I'm going to be personal. How well do you and Mrs. Akars know Van de Mark?"

"I don't know him at all," she returned. "Do you?"

"No, except for the evening here and a few encounters at the Inn. I imagine you know he's checked out temporarily."

Adrienne drew a deep breath. "You mean he's become a house guest some place?"

"I believe he has."

"And Craig Jones?"

"No, he's still where he belongs," he said dryly. "He's also a bona fide representative of a land company; that I do know."

"Dan," she turned to him with interest, "Friday night while I was away, some kind of celebration was held at my home, Were you there?"

"No, and not because I didn't try. I think Jones tried too. We didn't discuss it. We spent the evening in the inn lobby talking politics. Wasn't much fun. We agreed."

Caroline slipped out of the car and went out to the house, and Adrienne could ask why he had mentioned Van de Mark.

"Wanted to know how you felt about him."

"I don't. He is not the type I'd care to cultivate."

"Good. You know, Adrienne, if I had a lead on where he came from originally, I could have our office there check up on him. We have branches just about every place."

Like two photographs held up before her, Adrienne saw two envelopes: from different towns in different states: one addressed in the cramped hand of an elderly woman unaccustomed to writing; the other in a florid, careless hand.

"But," she asked, "is he using his own name?"

"Probably not, but the names of people writing him could be a means of establishing that."

"I know, and I'm sorry. It's been a lovely day. Thank you, and do have dinner with us some evening. I'll call you."

Caroline, to whom Adrienne had previously given a house key, had a hearth fire going when she entered.

"I could use a cup of tea," she said thoughtfully. "There's so much to wash down."

When they'd settled down she asked. "Addie, is Dan a Federal man?"

"Oh, I don't think so," she replied. "Why, Caroline? What made you think that?"

"I don't know," she admitted; "just something secretive about him. I liked him immensely. But—oh, well, you could tell by his mail if he were who he said he was."

"I'm not psychic," Adrienne insisted. "Besides, his mail doesn't come in to The Oaks. Nolga saw him picking it up from a private box in Lakeville, which could mean he doesn't intend to stay on here."

She had more to worry about than Dan Smith, and no one with whom to discuss it but the Judge.

Adrienne called him as soon as the mail was up to report that Craig Jones had not been present at the celebration.

"I'm relieved to hear that," the Judge said.

"Easier to deal with ethical people. Celebrating a deal not yet consummated is not ethical."

"Oh, but, Judge, " she protested, "the alternative is so much worse. What would she be celebrating? To me it means an emotional involvement with the other man."

"Good, good," he intoned. "Engagement party, perhaps? Fine solution."

"But—" sputtered Adrienne, then let her shoulders drop. Another of those letters had come to Frank Van de Mark in the morning mail, the writing that of an angry woman. Yet she couldn't tell the Judge she believed Van de Mark already married.

"Now you just let me handle this, Addie. And stop worrying. And Addie, there is one thing you can do without bruising your conscience. You can keep your eyes open even though you keep your mouth closed. For your own protection."

Gale winds were blowing the next morning when Adrienne started out. Caroline wanted to drive her but, as she left an hour later, Adrienne refused. "I'll enjoy it," she said.

"All right, but don't forget to duck if a tin roof comes sailing at you."

It wasn't a tin roof but a jeep that pulled alongside as she entered the highway.

Adrienne drew near as Hobart Hanson beckoned.

"Say, miss, could you do me a favor? Brakes

are slipping; taking the jeep over to get them fixed. Could you bring my mail out?"

"It isn't sorted yet."

"Doesn't matter; just bring anything that is." And then he added, "I'll wait back here near your door."

Thoughtfully Adrienne nodded. Having watched him stop, she knew there was nothing wrong with the jeep's brake. But for some reason he didn't want to wait for the post office to open.

Automatically she reviewed what had been in the small bundle she'd taken out: the usual letters from the usual women, one was from a young and one from an old woman; a thin letter from a crime magazine; some advertisements. She wondered who had written the letter he'd been reading outside the Tarryville post office.

"Thanks. I'll do something for you some day," he said quickly, and shot the jeep out into the street and up the hill.

Adrienne went in, smiling. She'd discovered something under the Hanson nose, the slow beginning of a moustache growing in patches and looking like bristles on the back of a mangy dog.

He must want it badly to put up with the process she thought. And the color was reddish blonde. Queer; she'd had the impression such hair as she'd seen had been dark.

She laughed about it with Collier; then he told her that often happened. There was no accounting for the chemistry of the body in some cases. Why, he knew a redhead with cotton white eyebrows.

This proved one of those days when the only people calling for mail were merchants or lonely people who couldn't stand the pressure of four walls after a long winter.

Adrienne could almost feel sorry for Vena Deere, who came in bustling, red with cold and argumentative.

"I have proof," she said, pounding the counter, "that an important letter left the city days ago. Now you go right in and search. You've placed it in the wrong box. Someone has taken it home with them. They'll never return it."

"If that might have happened," returned Adrienne wearily, "how did you receive proof?"

"By telephone, and I've a mind to charge you the toll cost."

"But if you talked to the party, then you know the contents of the letter. Wouldn't it be simpler to have them send a second letter as confirmation?"

"Never!" The ledge bounced at the slap of her hand. "I intend to use this as further proof this office needs—"

"I know: investigation."

When the outer door wheezed shut only because it couldn't slam, Adrienne said, "You know, that woman makes things happen. If she keeps on we're going to make one awful mistake."

"I know; she gives me a guilty conscience. But

we'll fool her. The mistake, if any, will be made at the other end."

Dotty Dougherty came in to ask loftily if Miss Akars had left Mrs. Akars' mail in her box or had taken it home. Miss Akars replied Miss Akars had left it in the box and would be happy to give it to Mrs. Dougherty if she would bring a note signed by Mrs. Akars.

"Women," sighed Collier happily as Dotty Dougherty flounced out.

Adrienne went for the mail: bills, one letter from her old home town and some advertisements. When the note was brought in, she handed it over.

Van de Mark came just after she'd left, sheafed through his letters, then came to the window to ask if they were sure all of his mail had been placed in his box.

"All that arrived," Collier told him. And when he had left, "Acted let down. Wonder what he was expecting?"

The next morning Adrienne wondered if she knew the answer. Frank Van de Mark received a letter postmarked from Nolga's old home town. It was in a cheap envelope, smudged and written by an illiterate hand.

Adrienne had an uncomfortable moment as she slipped it into his box. Surely, from the questions he'd hurled at her, he would know she sorted mail, might see this and wonder.

"Ever notice any mail going out of here with his name on it?" Collier asked in a musing tone.

"No," slowly Adrienne shook her head, "he must carry it to Lakeville. Perhaps because I am here and he's afraid I might tell Nolga."

It was good to go home that stormy night and find a warm house, a hot dinner and, above all, the warm friendly interest of Caroline.

"I'm glad I'm here," Caroline responded to Adrienne's spoken gratitude. "I'm enjoying it, and I know what a day-to-day strain you're under waiting for Nolga to act."

Later she said she must go to a teachers' meeting on Friday evening. There would be a dinner in the school cafeteria, then discussion of school problems.

"Hadn't you better plan to go to Gypsy's or somewhere?"

Adrienne reassured her. She'd been living in the house for twenty-four years. She'd been alone all night many times. And if Nolga chanced to read of the teachers' meeting and chose that time to visit, fine.

"I'll be glad to have it over."

She spent a restless night bracing herself for the inevitable showdown, then forgot it the next morning.

Two long, legal-looking letters came for Craig Jones, an airmail from an absent Oaks land owner.

Craig Jones was buying up land for The Belmont Land Company. Adrienne knew the long envelopes contained title guarantees.

She was alone when he came for his mail. This time, instead of hurrying out, he came to the window. "We haven't had our talk," he reproved her.

"We didn't need to; Judge Cobb talked for me. Surely not only he but your attorneys told you the will could not be broken."

"The contest," he said quietly, "was to free the property for sale. Conditions today are different. We are ready to buy. There is proof that both heirs would benefit."

She wanted to ask if they'd benefit as much from selling to him as from leasing to Ewa, but didn't. Besides, he forestalled this by saying, "It would be the bird in hand, Adrienne; not promises seven years away."

He left then, and she watched him, puzzled. He seemed changed; not so dynamic, not so eager to force her into joining Nolga and his company in breaking the will.

Burrows came in, and Adrienne knew sharp disappointment when he didn't even look at the window to greet her. Going out, he said, "Across the street," and then she saw Van de Mark again admiring a window display.

Adrienne had the uncomfortable feeling she was fighting a black fog, wind-driven. She wished a storm would blow in to clear the air.

The storm blew in Friday.

Nolga called Friday afternoon. "Adrienne, I want to see you this evening, alone."

"Fine. As you probably read in the *Courier*, Miss Johnson will be away. How about dinner?"

"Well, no." Was there a wistful note in the voice? "There are others coming, and with you working—"

"All right. Then whenever you're ready, come home."

Adrienne wanted very little dinner herself. She called the Judge before she left the post office, accepted the warning to watch her words and get in touch with him as soon as possible, then hurried home.

Arranging a bowl of japonica on the table, which held a number of cups, the coffee maker and a cake she'd bought, Adrienne wondered if her father could have seen ahead to a time when such arrangements for hospitality could be based upon such a theme.

If she only had a little more gumption, she thought irritably. But who expects an orchid to be a sunflower?

The orchid arrived looking like a violet, a shy, faded flower, bruised and shrinking from the cruel winds of adversity which had her half whipped.

"It's so good to be home," she crooned, drawing off her gloves and spreading tiny hands to the hearth fire.

"Shame you can't stay here." Frank Van de Mark threw the words at Adrienne, who refused the gambit.

She was waiting for Dotty and Craig Jones to appear, but it seemed only Frank was to be with Nolga.

Carefully he helped her out of her new spring topcoat, smoothed it, then spoiled the effect by tossing it to a chair where it slid in a heap to the floor.

"Better get on with it," he ordered.

"Frank, you tell her. I'm not up to it."

For once she was not acting. Adrienne saw the blue circles under her eyes, the frightened look within them. She had lost weight, and she seemed exhausted.

"Nothing to tell; just this, Addie. Nolga's fed up with you preventing her from getting what your father left her. Jones attorneys have an out on that will which will crack it the minute it shows up in court.

"It's not fair of you to want her to settle for peanuts so you can grab the swag."

He stopped, waiting for a commitment. Adrienne waited, frozen to silence.

"She's waited three years for you to grow up, taken care of you, worked for you, fed you, and for what? Not even a thank you."

Adrienne's eyes twinkled. She looked at Nolga and saw her peering through laced fingers.

"Somebody," Van de Mark started to stride around the small ell, "has to look out for her rights, and I'm the guy who's going to do it, see?"

Again silence fell.

"Well, say something, anything!" Nolga's voice was high, thin, hysterical.

"Nolga, Judge Cobb is wiser than I am. You know I am as interested in your welfare as in my own. I've let the Judge represent me so we will both benefit."

Something crashed as Frank wheeled. "Going to the car," he said, and banged out, slamming the door.

"Addie," Nolga was frightened, "you've got to sign, understand? If you care for me at all, you'll sign and not ask questions. Please, Addie!"

Chapter Eleven

Adrienne waited a moment, then said, "I feel a draught. Oh, I thought Frank closed that door."

He had. He'd opened it again to listen.

Swiftly she walked across, closed it again, and this time drew the bolt. "Frank can knock when he wants in," she said in a conversational tone. "I'd better have a carpenter in to look at the door; it must be off center or whatever doors are—"

"Addie," Nolga looked at the windows, "you will sign, won't you?"

"How much do you owe Frank, Nolga?"

There was an attempt at an indignant upthrust chin. "Five hundred. But we're going to be married, so it isn't a debt."

"I'll raise the five hundred. About signing, do you need to tell him everything? I want to meet you at Judge Cobb's office tomorrow afternoon. Can you? Alone?"

"Not alone. Addie, can you really—I mean the five hundred?"

"Definitely."

"He's not asking for it."

"Nolga, did you give him a note when you borrowed the money? And have you any of it left?"

"Oh, there he is knocking. No, I didn't. Oh, do let him in, Addie."

Adrienne walked over to the door, pulled the slide bolt and smiled at Van de Mark. "Frank, I wish you'd look at this door. It doesn't seem to stay closed, and while winter's over—"

She hadn't fooled him. Nor did she like him any better for the crooked, knowing smile he gave her.

"All fixed up?" he asked.

"I've arranged to meet Nolga tomorrow at Judge Cobb's. I imagine we can catch Craig Jones and have him meet us there."

"Aha," the voice was like the rubbing of palms, "that's more like it. You've had this little girl badly upset, chasing her out of her home and all that."

Adrienne let that pass, watching Nolga. She fluttered her hands at Frank and gave Adrienne an appealing look.

"Why don't you stay tonight and go in with me tomorrow?" she asked suddenly.

Frank answered for her. Nolga's car was at Dotty's; besides, it was no way to treat a friend like Mrs. Dougherty.

Adrienne followed them to the side door. Nolga ran ahead to get into Frank's car, but Frank waited a moment, adjusting his hat to the exact slant he wanted.

"By the way," he said, "I'm changing my address to Lakeville." Still he waited, then added, "Now," and went on.

"Oh, Frank," she called after him, "you'd better send a change of address card. We're not allowed to transfer by word of mouth."

She called the Judge as soon as she saw the car headlights turn south onto the Lakeville highway. "I'm afraid to talk," she said. "I wouldn't put it past one of them to drive on while the other waited. I'll call in the morning."

When Caroline came in bubbling with excitement (the Ag teacher had asked her for a date), she found Adrienne huddled over the fire. "That bad?" she asked.

Adrienne nodded but waited until they were upstairs before she answered.

"I don't know how bad, but I'm even more worried than I've been. And I don't know what to do about it."

Caroline suggested a sleeping pill so she'd be mentally alert the next day, but Adrienne refused. She wanted to do some sharp thinking tonight.

Wrapped in a warm robe, she curled into a chair before the west windows, looking out on the spangled hills and shore that was Lakeville.

If there was only someone she could talk to, trust to go down and investigate before she had to deal with Frank.

Dan Smith? He was interested. But he'd be the kind to investigate and say nothing.

Red Burrows? She shrank from exposing Nolga's life to him.

Craig Jones?

Adrienne glanced at her bedside clock. Eleven. The Oaks rolled up its sidewalks at nine-thirty week days, yet she went to the telephone and called, praying the inn operator wouldn't listen in.

"Nolga has been here," she told him. "I need to talk to someone, and you're elected. Could you come over?"

"Yes, and quietly. Front door?"

He came quietly, walking from the inn, tapping at the door and coming in to sit in the dark of the big hall.

"Van de Mark?" he asked.

"How did you know?"

"Sometimes men have intuitions. How far has that romance gone, Addie?"

"I don't think it's a romance, Craig. I'm sure Frank is trying some kind of blackmail on Nolga. She's frightened. He pretended to let us talk alone together but left the door open, or reopened it. I noticed, bolted it, and he didn't like it."

She couldn't tell him about the letter that had come to Frank; she could say she had "reason to believe he has dug up some scandal about Nolga."

"That little nitwit in a scandal?" he said affectionately. "If she was in one, she was framed. But the poor kid would be scared. What can I do?"

"Have you any contacts in her home town? Anyone you can trust who'd quietly check and find out what it was?"

He thought a moment. "I'll do better than that. Plane through the county seat from the north at three o'clock. I'll go down myself. Have you any leads at all, any names?"

She wrote the two names she remembered—they were both in the telephone book—and then she thought of him. "Oh, Craig, I'm asking you to do something to help me, and I'm not doing a thing to help you."

"I'll get along," he assured her. "Now I have to hop. Sit steady and don't talk. If Frank thinks you're signing up tomorrow, he won't be able to blame you if I don't show up. I'll wire from the city I was called away on business. Have to stop there for a change of planes anyway. Now get some sleep."

She did, and without a sleeping pill, wondering what there was about a shrewd promoter like Craig to give her such a sense of confidence.

Saturday morning it was Rod Burrows who stood before the windows across from the post office, finally coming in during a quiet moment.

"Do I have to spend another Sunday alone?" he asked. "Couldn't we slip away some place?"

Adrienne didn't know how, and now especially

she had to be careful not to antagonize Van de Mark further.

"Say, I have a thought. Suppose you and the young lady staying with you come to the inn for dinner. I'll come over to your table and you'll be my guests. Then if the coast is clear we'll go for a drive.

"Let's" breathed Adrienne. "I'm developing nerves. Rod, how long will your company wait?"

"Don't worry about that."

She went to her conference that afternoon in better spirits.

"I'll shop and come back to the car, " Caroline said, "but don't feel you have to hurry. I may even have some servicing done on it."

The meeting in Judge Cobb's office was an anticlimax. Nolga, looking even worse than she had the night before, was clinging to Frank's arm, and for once the Judge allowed him to come into the office.

"Well now," the Judge beamed on them, "seems one of our party has flown. Wire here from Craig Jones." He leaned across and handed it to Adrienne, who read it and passed it on to Nolga. Frank almost snatched it from her.

But Adrienne remembered the message: "Regret unable to keep appointment; crisis on another matter. Will wire time of return. Attorney will accompany me. Please hold signing of papers until he has received them."

Nolga gave a faint cry and slid down in her chair.

"Now see what you've done to her," Frank snapped. Adrienne and the Judge's secretary worked over her a moment while Cobb said judicially, "Gossip says the Dougherty house has turned into a night club. Probably isn't getting any rest."

"Nolga," Adrienne said as her stepmother's eyes opened, "why don't you come home?"

"She will not. I'll take her to the hospital. That's the place for her; the things she has to put up with around you people."

"Hospital beds are at a premium. I doubt if she's sick enough to warrant one," said Cobb. "What's that?"

Money," whispered Nolga. "Who'd pay for it?"

"The estate!" said Frank.

"If the estate chooses the hospital and the attending doctor," Cobb flung back at him, and reached for the telephone.

As the Judge talked to Dr. "Angel," Frank muttered something about Nolga being exposed to people who'd upset her.

"Frank," Adrienne said earnestly, "I give you my word I won't try to visit her."

"We'll do better than that," stated Judge Cobb. "Angel and I will see no one visits her for at least a week. Dotty Dougherty called him and said Mrs.

Akars was on the verge of a nervous breakdown. Now, young man, satisfied?"

"No mail," he looked at Adrienne, and no visitors. All right, but I'll take her there."

"Fine, you do that," agreed Cobb. "I'll follow and make the financial arrangements."

Caroline returned to the car to find Adrienne looking "like a wet dish rag."

"Oh, dear, and me with my date tonight," cried Caroline. "With Van de Mark on the loose, I don't think you should stay there alone. What can we do?"

Well, there was one man left, Dan Smith. Adrienne telephoned him as soon as she reached home.

"Make a deal with you," he agreed. "Not that I won't enjoy spending the evening here. But I have a thing about that Van de Mark. I have a good hunch he'll show up to give you a bad time. Fine, I'll be there. But I want his fingerprints. Will you help me?"

Dan Smith arrived, as had Craig Jones, on foot. Adrienne had drawn the drapes against the gentle rain falling outside. The three had a quiet dinner.

"This place grows on one," Smith remarked. "It won't be easy for you to give it up."

"I did, six years ago," Adrienne said.

When Frank had not appeared by ten o'clock, Dan asked how well he knew the house.

"I don't know," Adrienne admitted. "He visited

here when I wasn't home. I imagine Nolga took him around"

"Then, Caroline, how about you going up and turning on the light in your room?"

Ten minutes after the light went on Van de Mark knocked at the door.

"Evening. Thought I'd have a little talk with you, Addie," he said.

"Fine; come in. How is Nolga?"

"A lot you care. Look, Addie," he paused halfway to the ell, "you can cut the act with me. I know women. You didn't like your Dad marrying a kid like her and you still don't like it. But I'm here to tell you I'm sticking around to see she gets what's coming to her."

"As her future husband?"

He waited a moment. "What's wrong with that?" Adrienne shrugged, "I think it's most commendable. Now what was it you wanted to talk about?"

"Jones being called away is not going to make any difference in your signing. And don't count on Nolga not getting out of the hospital on time. She will. She knows what is good for . . . Oh, hello, Smith. Didn't know you were here."

"Nice change from hotel life," Smith said easily. "Come over where it's warm. Addie, might be an idea to open that bottle I brought over. Frank here looks chilled through."

Adrienne brought the drinks in tall smooth

mugs, without handles, while Dan talked of being held up by snow in the pass.

The climate has gone haywire," he insisted. "Snow comes so late the game stays in the hills, then lasts until summer is well along. You do any hunting?"

"Yes and no," replied Frank with his sly, secret smile.

He had one drink, then decided he'd be getting along. Nice seeing Smith. Did he come over often?

"Yes," Dan said. "I'm thinking of moving in. There've been prowlers around." He paused. Frank had stiffened. "With Caroline here it might be a good idea to have a man handy with a gun on the premises."

"Yeah," Frank agreed, "maybe."

"How about driving me back to the inn for my bag?"

Adrienne let them out, bolted the door, then hurried toward the hall to find Caroline waiting.

"That idea I like," Caroline stated. "Addie, what's wrong? That Frank person gives me the jitters."

There was a big master bedroom on the first floor. Both girls hurried to make it comfortable, even building a fire in the small iron stove that the climate demanded.

Frank returned with Dan to stand around and finally say, "Come to think of it, two men would be better than one. What say I move in, too?"

"That would put too much of a strain on the town gossips," Dan said quickly.

"You'll be moving in for good soon, won't you, Frank?"

"Here, are you kidding? Me and Nolga will take off for a place they don't use tombstones for name plates."

He left and Dan softly said, "Wonder if the lad is running out of ready cash?"

Adrienne wondered about Nolga and the five hundred.

"I'll talk to you in the morning," Dan said. "And, Addie, I didn't really check out. I'll have my meals at the inn. You don't mind me sleeping here?"

"We'll sleep," Adrienne said. And Caroline joined in, "But you will have breakfast with us tomorrow? It's Sunday, you know."

The gentle rain gave in to the advancing sun and turned the world into rainbows that wound in mist through the trees and across the lake.

Adrienne, setting the breakfast table, looked up to where a golden glint on a hill across the lake burnished the sun room of Dr. Angel's hospital. Nolga was safe there, but was she resting?

And here she herself was wasting time that might be spent with Rod.

"What did you say?" asked Caroline.

"I think I said I wondered why I objected to

being bored last winter. This nervous strain isn't fun. Oh, good morning, Dan."

They talked at breakfast. Dan said he'd like to take the mug Van de Mark had used the previous evening down to the county seat. Would they like to go along for the ride?

Adrienne mentioned the date with Burrows, and Dan called him. If they left immediately they wouldn't be seen; they'd plan to return after dark. He doubted Frank would be hovering around.

He was wrong. When they drove in, Frank's car was in the driveway, his luggage beside the door.

Chapter Twelve

In the moment of silence that fell, Adrienne felt a sense of defeat. This was the worst crisis she had had to face. Coming at the end of the most perfect day she had ever enjoyed, it was a bitter climax.

"I'll take care of this," Dan snapped.

"No," Adrienne reached forward to place a detaining hand on his shoulder, "I'm not in a position to let you. Wait, Dan, until we know."

"But you girls can't live there with that man in the same house" Rod remarked reasonably, "not even with Dan standing guard. You'll have to give him the boot."

"I don't think we can," Adrienne said softly. "Half of that house is Nolga's. I'm sure he'll have a note from Nolga, probably prearranged, saying he's to be a guest there."

"I think the guy is broke," Dan mused. "Say, I have it. I didn't give up my room at the inn. Rod, you do a vanishing act. I'll take the girls in to pick up some clothes, then let them take my room. We'll talk there, later."

They let Dan go toward the house first. Frank was ready for him.

"Mrs. Akars sent me over," Frank announced. "Had Dr. Angel, as you call him, phone Mrs. Dougherty. She wants someone on the premises who has her interests at heart. Lot of valuable stuff in here."

"I see," Dan said smoothly. "Of course you know village gossip. One man might stay; two is out of the question. I'll stay on to look after Miss Akars' interests, and she and Miss Johnson can take my room at the hotel. I suppose you have a key."

"I sure have; just didn't chance using it before I talked to Addie. Didn't intend her having me up for breaking and entering."

"All right, I'll call the girls."

"Who's going to do the cooking?" Frank asked.

"That I wouldn't know. I have my meals at the inn or wherever mealtime finds me. Addie, come on."

Frank was the first one in. Arrogantly he stalked along the hall and up the stairs to Nolga's room.

"I'll be within call," Dan told Addie as she and Caroline followed to pack their bags.

As they anticipated, Frank was at the door of Adrienne's room soon after she entered.

"This is plain foolishness," he stated. "No need for you to run up bills so's this guy can have it soft here. I can keep an eye on you as good as he can."

Adrienne turned toward him. "Let's face this, Frank. I have no reason to like you. You have been rude, unfair and unjust. I don't intend to jeopardize my job by letting you keep me upset."

"You and your job," he sneered. "Whata laugh! And don't think Danny boy is going to pull anything funny. Not with me."

Adrienne returned to her work. In another moment Frank moved into the room. "Look, Addie, no need of us being enemies. I admit I've been edgy. I'm like that, high-strung. Fell for little Nolga, saw she was getting a raw deal and—well, you know."

Caroline, having little to pack, was ready and came in, as a signal for Frank to leave. Adrienne soon joined her.

They heard the telephone shrill, heard Dan's voice, then went down, but he didn't mention the caller until they were in the car.

"That was Dotty Dougherty calling. I told her I was taking you to the inn, and she said, 'Oh-oh, so the little bounder moved in. I kicked him out of here.' She's going to call you there."

Rod was waiting for them in the lobby. He had rented a sitting room to use as an office and asked the girls to come up after they'd checked into their room. He'd have coffee sent up.

"Addie," Caroline protested when they were alone, "I should go back to my boardinghouse."

"Not unless it will jeopardize your job."

"With Clive and Ed Weaver on the board? Hardly. But you'd have more—"

"—Nerve tension. Can't you imagine the relief of talking things out with you?"

"Such as?"

"Right now, can't you imagine how I feel about leaving the house that's been home all of my life exposed to Frank?"

Dotty Dougherty's call came before they left the room. Dotty was apologetic. "Addie," she said in her abrupt way, "you have more sense than I gave you credit for." She went on about Nolga and Frank Van de Mark, and Adrienne let her talk. She remembered Dotty making quite a play for Frank that first evening at the house.

She also said in view of the way Nolga acted around the man, she'd felt, as a friend, she should talk to Dr. Angel, arrange for Nolga to be kept away from him until she came to her senses. Naturally she took credit for the coup.

"Then I had to get rid of my star boarder."

Adrienne was laughing when the two girls joined the men in Rod's "office." She would, she confessed, have enjoyed watching the three Dougherty women get rid of the one Van de Mark man.

"How long does this have to go on?" Rod asked.

Dan said he hoped to have a run-down on the fingerprints before too long.

"And by the way," asked Caroline, "can just anyone walk into police headquarters, ask for and receive the service you received?"

Dan waited a moment before he replied. "I haven't lied to any of you. I am with the insurance company I mentioned. I just failed to tell you which branch. I know you'll keep this a secret."

"You're not after Van de Mark? Rod asked with sudden concern.

"No, definitely not. He is very small pumpkins. I am, as I said, sitting it out until the pass opens."

Rod relaxed. "I was about to suggest I join you at the Akars house. Guess, however, you know how to handle him."

"I think so. I think he's been up against the law enough to sense I'm in with them. I doubt he'll try to prove it one way or another. Right now he's trying to sit it out until Mrs. Akars has a settlement."

After coffee and cakes had been brought in and the waiter had departed, Rod looked at Adrienne. "You're very thoughtful. Want to tell us?"

"Yes and no. I'm puzzled about this. You, Rod, Dan, Craig Jones and Frank Van de Mark arrived at The Oaks almost on the same day. That is too many to be a coincidence."

"Weather," Dan said, "as far as I'm concerned."

"I think Jones and I would give the same answer. I wasn't ready to start action until the snow was off the land I wanted to see. The lake had a chinook wind the week before. I followed it. Jones, knowing the time I was leaving, got the lead out of his shoes and met me here, fater a fashion.

"Until someone from our firm became actively interested, there was no assurance we would buy, thus no assurance his firm would benefit from anything they bought."

"And that leaves Van de Mark the only enigma," Caroline contributed.

"The man too many," murmured Adrienne.

Dan decided he needed cigarets, and Caroline thought she wanted a candy bar or two; she'd go down to the lobby with him.

Adrienne went to the window to look across the lake to the beacon of light on the hill, Dr. Angel's hospital.

"Addie," Rod was beside her, following her gaze, "how can a nice woman like Mrs. Akars become involved with a man like Van de Mark? You couldn't."

"No," admitted Adrienne ruefully. "I work in a post office."

She explained a little about life in a small post office. A person would have to be very stupid not to learn how to judge character.

"More than that," he grasped the idea quickly, "you learn what's going on in individuals' lives.

You know more about Van de Mark than you're telling."

"I don't know; I surmise."

"You could have helped Dan run down his background, which means helping yourself where the estate is concerned."

"And you—"

"And me, all of us. But you haven't."

"I couldn't, Rod. My word is too important to me, my belief in our post office system too firm. I'm sorry."

"Sorry!"

She heard the word, then heard Caroline and Dan returning. She wondered what more he would have said, what he had meant.

He managed a final word with her. "The happiest day I've ever had, Addie."

The words carried her through the difficult hour before she slept. Caroline had left her the twin bed near the window, and she lay looking uphill to the house lights of The Oaks. Tonight she felt some of the security these symbolized. She hadn't been left completely alone to face this.

Frank was blackmailing Nolga in some way. But Craig would find the cause and correct it. She had confidence in him.

Her beloved home was at the mercy of Frank, but Dan was there. Now that he'd identified himself as an investigator, a former law officer, she knew Frank was playing for stakes too high to risk exposure through a man he intuitively knew to be on the other side.

And there was Rod. Queer how a square face and an IBM mind could convey so much tenderness.

Adrienne was up long before the others. It was sheer luxury to bathe and dress in a warm room, go down to a cheerful dining room and have breakfast placed before her.

There was little to interest her in the mail until, passing Dan's box, she saw a letter there.

For a long time she stood staring at it, longing to take it out, to hold it, to study the writing, the postmark, to seek by some ethical means to learn the identity of the sender, the relationship, the contents.

And then she turned away. Collier had opened the foyer door. Now Adrienne opened the first stamp window, to be greeted by Vena Deere.

"Mr. Collier, please. I don't care to have you wait on me. There are limits to what the public must endure. A girl, living in a big house alone with a man."

"Two men," murmured Adrienne absently.

"Two!" The woman's voice rose.

"And two girls," Collier came up, "living at the inn, not at the house. Now what do you want this morning, Mrs. Deere?"

"Nothing," she stated, "nothing at all. I am taking my business to Lakeville."

"A man can hope," muttered Collier as he turned away. "Addie, where does that woman pick up information?"

"She doesn't," sighed Adrienne. "She picks up bits others have discarded as worthless and weaves them into a pattern of her own."

After the early rush was over Addie called the hospital and was put through to the ward nurse.

"I'm so glad you called," the woman said. "Mrs. Akars had such a restless night we resorted to measures to induce relaxation. She says she has to tell you something which will explain why she has acted as she has."

"Oh, that," Adrienne replied. "Tell her I investigated and learned all about it, to forget it. It's all in the past. She needn't worry about it. Tell her all she needs to do is rest and grow strong; by the time the doctor releases her all of her problems will be run out of town."

The nurse had written down the message. Now she read it back.

Dr. Angel called at noon. "Dr. Akars?" he inquired blithely. "That mental medication you sent over did wonders. Our girl is sitting up begging for food. But she asked me a peculiar favor. I was to tell anyone who called that she was in too serious a condition to talk."

"Hurrah," said Adrienne. "Did you agree?"

"I did."

"Oh, and, Doctor, if she recovers so rapidly you

have to oust her from a needed bed, will you find a place for her there? I'll pay her room and board."

"I think work is indicated. I'll give her a job that will keep her out of circulation until you give the word."

Adrienne sat back, relieved. Nolga had finally admitted she needed help to free her from Frank.

In another moment Adrienne was up, pacing the floor. She remembered what she had told the nurse and now she realized what Nolga had read into it. She, Adrienne, had referred to the immediate past, to their relationship as stepdaughter and stepmother. Nolga, in her own mind, had but one past, the one Craig was investigating.

Adrienne began counting days. Craig had left Friday night or early Saturday morning. He would have reached Nolga's home town that afternoon, taking a bus in from the nearest airport.

How long would it take him to run down the information he sought?

And how long before Dan received a report?

Dan's full report came on Wednesday. He called it disappointing.

"Just a small time confidence man," he mourned.

"But that is what you thought him," Adrienne insisted.

"I know. I'd hoped someone was looking for him. As far as the law's concerned, he's clean. He hasn't much of a record; served a year in '50 for petty theft. Some widow brought the charge. He'd borrowed the money from her, he said.

"His racket is playing up to widows for stakes, always promising marriage."

"Is he married?" Adrienne asked.

"Doesn't say. No occasion to keep track of his marital status. But he has been. Last one recorded in '58, to a Janine Jeffers of Pottsville, Pennsylvania."

He's married, Adrienne thought. He can't marry Nolga; he can only go through the pretense while he attempts to borrow money from her. He's counted on the blackmail to keep her from prosecuting him after he leaves. I know he's married; that one woman writes from Pottsville.

And then she chanced to look at Dan's face. It was grim, yet there was an air of triumph.

"Dan," Adrienne spoke softly, Tessie having come into the rear of the post office, "could you find out for sure about his marriage?"

He looked at her, interested. "Yes. It will take a little while. I've maps at the hotel. I'll check tonight and find our nearest office. Talk to you later."

"How are you two getting along?" she ventured.

"Don't see much of him. He evidently sleeps until long after I've gone. I've noticed signs of cooking and cleaning up in the kitchen, not too well done. Don't know where he spends his days." He tipped his hat and left.

Rod came in. "Mind bringing my late mail?" he asked. "See you at dinner?"

Tessie watched. "Honestly, Add, for a girl with as many good-looking men in your life as you have, you don't seem very happy."

"That's the trouble. I've one too many."

But she didn't explain.

The late mail came in. Adrienne's mind was focused on Rod's mail. His request that she bring it to the hotel was his way of saying he was convinced of her integrity.

She wondered how he would feel toward her if Craig learned Nolga had been mixed up in some unsavory scandal.

"My, but you're getting nervous," declared Tessie, "I never saw you drop mail before.

"I know." She stopped and picked it up.

"Here's an airmail special for that man staying at your house."

"I'll take that," said Frank Van de Mark from the window.

He opened it, read it, then called to Adrienne, "Letter from my sister. Thought you might be getting ideas about my mail. See—"

"I don't care to see your mail," Adrienne said stiffly, but her eye had recorded a last line: "Jan's

144

getting in my hair; you should have done more than divorce her. Love, Sis."

A sister lived in the same town as her sister-in-law. "Now about the money I loaned Nolga, I could use a little of it—two or three hundred."

Chapter Thirteen

The money he had loaned Nolga.

Tessie had heard. Adrienne was aware of a break in the rhythm of her work, then heard it pick up. Better Tessie than anyone else.

"Frank, I don't carry that kind of money on me. You should have come earlier, bringing Nolga's note so I could borrow from the bank."

"Borrow?" He seemed a little surprised. "I didn't ask for a note. Great guns, Addie, Nolga's my fiancée. As for waiting this late, I thought there'd be a draft in this letter. Sister was supposed to send it. Some kind of a holiday there. She'll get it off right away, but the weekend's coming up."

Not that soon, thought Adrienne.

She didn't doubt Nolga had borrowed from him, knowing her stepmother. But how much?

"Wait." She went to her handbag and counted the few bills there, then walked back with all but five dollars. "Here is forty, Frank; it's all I have, and I want a receipt."

"A receipt, among friends?" he cried.

"With money it's a safe way to keep on being

146

friends," she stated, typed out a receipt and handed it to him to sign before she gave him the money.

She was still standing at the window when he drove off. Another car came in, headlights flashing on the wall, attracting her.

"Tessie, I swear that Man Wanted up there is alive. His beard grows daily."

"Collier should tack them up so high the school kids can't reach them. Any new ones in the gallery?"

Adrienne blessed Tessie for passing off Frank's visit without comment, and replied, "Just one. Some fellow who chose small boardinghouses for his field of activity. He'd watch incoming mail, usually left on a stand table in the hall, slit the envelopes and remove the contents, if money.

"He operated in several boardinghouses; then temptation became too much for him. He cashed some money orders. Now Uncle Sam wants to offer him a private room and board."

They closed up the post office and walked out. Adrienne almost into the arms of The Oaks lone cab driver.

"I'm to take you to the inn," he said. "Friend of yours said you looked tired out."

Willingly Adrienne got into the cab and leaned back, watching the skyline as they drove into a muddy sunset.

Going into the inn, she found the manager relieving the desk clerk. "You look tired, Miss

Addie," he commented as he handed her the key. "Maybe this will cheer you up." And he slipped a hotel envelope into her hand.

She read it as she walked toward the elevator, then turned and looked out. Muddy sunset? Something had happened. Now the sky was golden apricot, the young leaves of trees between the inn and the lake a jet black filigree.

For Rod had written, "Dan has to drive in to the county seat and Caroline's going along for the ride. Will you please be my guest? I've ordered dinner sent up to the 'office.' Call me when you're ready."

Time to shower. Time to don the dress Gypsy had "whipped up" for her because she, Gypsy, had seen this print and felt it needed Adrienne. It was the soft after-glow of palest apricot with a jet black over-design; a pleated hair band of the apricot bound back her hair.

She "let it down." There was something relaxing about having it fall softly to her shoulders.

Adrienne telephoned, then walked down to Rod's suite. When he opened the door, she thought, this is what I've dreamed of on dreary nights. A small fire on the hearth, a table for two with flowers and lighted tapers. Above all a man such as Rod, waiting.

"It's lovely," she said, handing him his mail.

"I had a little trouble restraining the maître d'hôtel. He wanted flowers all over the place and had some concoction thought up for dinner. I chose that. Caroline tattled; said you weren't eating enough."

"Just nerves; I'm even dropping things. I'm ashamed."

"You needn't be; you've been under quite a strain. You would rather dine up here, wouldn't you?"

She laughed. "Yes. The manager made it so obvious I had his blessing—"

Adrienne hadn't the faintest idea what she was eating until she came to liver, and then she revolted.

"Try it; it's cooked in wine vinegar. You need it. You've lost that lovely color I saw the first day."

Adrienne stared in shocked surprise. "I didn't know you *saw* me that first day."

"Oh, yes. If you can put up with a man who looks like me going poetic on you, you resembled one of those blossoms that don't come out all at once. You know the kind. They wear green overcoats and stick their noses out to try out the weather before they risk it."

Adrienne laughed unhappily.

"Then when you returned," she offered, "you found me completely changed. That was disappointment."

"Oh, no, it wasn't. I'd never have had the nerve to ask your 'sister' for a date. Too young, for one thing; too dead-pan. She sized me up, made me feel she knew more about me than I knew about myself."

"Rod, you're a perfect host, but you're giving me a split personality."

"Good. At least I held your interest until you ate the liver. Max," he called out, "you can bring in the chops now."

The waiter came in, stared at Adrienne's plate and shook his head. "I'd never've believed it, sir. Time and again I've seen Mr. Akars try, when she was a little tyke."

"Mr. Burrows used hypnosis, Max," Adrienne said.

Perhaps it was hypnosis which gave such enchantment to the evening. Not a word was said about the Akars' land, about Ewa, the Belmont Land Company, Nolga or Frank.

Adrienne relaxed in a deep chair, eyelids heavy, then found herself propelled out. "Exactly what I wanted," said Rod. "Now slip into bed before you wake up. See you in the morning."

In the morning she was both deeply ashamed and deeply depressed. Rod had been wonderful. However, his treatment had been that of physician who recognized her need of rest, not a man interested in her emotionally.

And of course she overslept and had to rush off to work, planning to have coffee sent in from the cafe.

"Pussycat" Paul, the soft-footed man of The Oaks who washed all windows, had just finished the great sheets of glass that enclosed the foyer as Adrienne went out to unlock.

"Seems to me," he was looking up at the Rogues' Gallery, "Mr Collier ought to put up replacements. What those kids won't do."

Adrienne followed his glance and laughed a little. That last circular, the boardinghouse letter lifter, had developed a curly moustache and chin whiskers.

"Oh, well," Pussyfoot picked up his long-handled mop and squeegee, " 'tain't likely we'd have any of them around here."

Adrienne nodded, then met the gaze of the man whose beard had grown steadily for months until she could hardly remember what he had looked like originally.

Her interest piqued, she moved up to read the descripton of the mail robber:

> Five foot eleven, receding hairline, blond hair, greyish-green eyes. No distinguishing marks.

She turned away, looked at the latest circular. That man did have distinguishing marks, now that the youngsters were through with him.

The mail was light that morning. There was a letter for the Lakeville woman, a thin one. The romance was growing thin. Soon the letters would stop.

It was then such a woman would usually come to the window to ask anxiously, "Are you sure you couldn't have put it in another box by mistake?"

Adrienne sighed. Why didn't these older women realize forbidden fruit grew bitter with age?

Ah, good. In the case of the two taking the same correspondence course, *he* had driven *her* to the post office. Imagine a book acting as an arrow. Adrienne felt like an out-sized cupid.

Now if she could just find a solution to Miss Pinderson.

Ha, why not? Mickey Mahoney needed work this summer, and Miss Pinderson, who sometimes opened her house to an overflow of vacationers, always hired some youngster. Mickey only came down out of space during English lessons. English wasn't "for the birds"; birds he could understand. It was for landlubbers, people who never took their eyes off the earth.

She could afford to keep him on through the winter.

"Here comes that man again," said Collier.

Adrienne felt a shiver of apprehension as Frank Van de Mart walked in, went to his box, found nothing and came to the window.

"What time you going to the bank?" he asked in a low voice.

"I'm not," Adrienne said, hoping he didn't hear her convulsive swallow. "I gave you all I had."

"Nothing wrong with your credit, is there? Now look, Addie, I loaned Nolga the money I had with me. She was short because you'd been bleeding her ever since your Dad died. Well, it's time to pay up."

"Frank, I—" Oh, what could she tell him; what excuse could she give? And she must not give him more until she was able to worm the truth out of Nolga, find out how much Frank had given her.

Suddenly an idea flashed into her mind. "Can you wait until this evening," she asked, "or even this noon? I can borrow from Dan Smith. When I tell him the circumstances—"

She got no further. With a savage, "Skip it and keep your mouth shut," he left.

He didn't go far. As soon as Collier left to cross the street to the bank he was back.

"Did you tell *him* what I said?" he asked.

"I didn't have to," Adrienne replied wearily. "Voices carry in here."

"What did he say?"

"Frank, this is a business office. If you want to go into this, come to the hotel tonight."

For probably the only time in the years she had known her, Adrienne welcomed Vena Deere, who chose that moment to walk in, sniff suspiciously, then stand and wait until Frank left.

"I don't like that man. What did he want?" she demanded.

Adrienne replied, "Is there something I can do for you?"

Vena Deere spoke her mind. People who used government offices to carry on flirtations should be reported. The "carryings on" she'd seen would alert the men in the—

"Higher echelons," Adrienne absently chanted with her, though the idea of a flirtation with Frank was so repugnant she almost gagged.

Alone again, she telephoned the hospital to ask for the ward nurse.

"Yes, Addie," the nurse replied. "He's tried every means of getting in. In fact, Dr. Angel called the Judge last night. We've taken care of the situation."

Adrienne wasn't to know how, but she was satisfied.

That night she let mail slither through her hands like water, but neither Tess nor Mr. Collier made any comment. Adrienne did. "This must stop," she told herself sharply.

"Here, take the packages," said Collier. "Easier to handle."

Willingly Adrienne switched her routine, but with the first package, fumbled and dropped it to the cement floor. She had seen "Dorothy's Beauty Salon" in one corner; the address, "Mrs. Harriette Hanson, Box 1180, The Oaks."

"Oh-oh," Collier, bending over to retrieve the small parcel, frowned, "must be ink. Those people didn't wrap this properly. Well, we'll send it back."

"I'll take care of it," Adrienne insisted. "Let me take it to the washroom."

Slipping a piece of cardboard under it, she walked carefully until she reached the room, then as carefully completed the unwrapping.

The label was still visible. The bottle had contained hair dye "guaranteed not to wash out."

It was comedy relief. Adrienne thought of that funny little moustache Hobart Hanson had been growing. She didn't blame him for wanting to cover it. And of course no man could blatantly go to a counter and ask for dye. There were many dyes he could have picked up with no comment, but these did wash out. And unless he wanted to go around with a dirty face, it would mean constant applications.

The others, finding her happy, went their way, and Adrienne went on with her thoughts. Imagine the great Hobart Hanson having coffee in some public place, starting out with a black moustache and, when he was through, having a half-moon of blond where the black should have been.

Oh, well, soon the weather would be so warm he'd have to wear a hat instead of a cap or go bareheaded; then she could tell if his hair matched his moustache. Or would he dye that too?

Why should a man dye his hair?

Adrienne went out of the post office that night so fast she had to return to check the doors.

She almost ran to the inn. The only reason she didn't was because she saw Frank's car. In it Frank sat watching her. And because she was afraid he'd slide up and demand to take her, she went into the market, out through the back door and to the inn by a roundabout way.

Dan Smith was in the lobby. So was Rod, but she didn't see him. "Dan," she whispered when he came up, shocked at her white face, "I must talk to you, alone."

She didn't see the expression on Rod's face as he walked away; it was a combination of resignation and pain.

"Dan," when they were in a window embrasure, she spoke, "have you a photograph of the man you're looking for?"

He was instantly alert. "Circular. Yes."

"I must see it."

"Come on."

The elevator seemed to crawl. When they reached the room Adrienne was occupying, Dan went to the one drawer he'd retained and from it took a locked brief case. In the false back was a list of papers.

Anxiously Adrienne watched as he drew these out.

"This help?" He handed her a circular, and she stared down, puzzled.

This couldn't be the same one that hung on the post office wall; this man was wanted for bank robbery. Yet if she could remember what that photograph looked like, months ago—

"Dan, when was this robbery committed?"

"The same day this same man, with two accomplices, robbed a small post office. Last July."

"Dan, Frank wasn't one of them? No, he couldn't have been, or hadn't they a description?"

"He wasn't. The other two were caught and tucked into Federal prison. Addie, have you seen this man?"

"I'm not sure. Wait." She went to her bag, drew out small scissors; then she went to a drawer to take a band of ribbon out. Carefully she fashioned a tiny cap, then went back to lay the circular flat on the desk and fit the cap to the head.

The receding hairline was gone. The man who called himself Hobart Hanson, a writer of true crime stories, stared back at her from the photograph.

"Addie!"

But Addie was recalling the circular on the post office wall. What were the instructions? Weren't they always the same? Could she remember them?

Chapter Fourteen

Adrienne's photographic memory supplied the answer, the words, "Cause immediate arrest and notify the following..."

Bank robbery. Banks were insured against robbery (rather loss of money) by some large general insurance company. Dan Smith obviously worked in the department assigned to such investigations. He would know how to "cause immediate arrest."

"Yes," the word slipped out, "but I want Mr. Collier in on this."

Dan sighed. "Naturally. And the Federals have the first claim. At that, I won't be sorry to have a hand. Now, how can we have a conference with him without having little Frankie watching."

"Frank Van de Mark?" Having had Dan dispose of him as an accomplice, Adrienne was surprised.

"The term Frank served was spent in the same county jail that housed our Hobart Hanson, whose name incidentally is neither Hobart nor Hanson. Nor is Frank's name Van de Mark. He added the 'Van' and the 'de' and left off the 'inson.' Our Hanson was serving a minor sentence. He branched into big time afterwards.

"Now about Collier—"

Adrienne telephoned to say, "Can you come to the inn in such a way anyone watching will not know you've come to see me? It's terribly important."

"Knowing you, yes. I have it. Carter's there. I'll ask for him, then come to your room. What's the number?

The waiting time seemed endless. Adrienne's thoughts turned to Frank Van de Mark, or Markinson.

"Dan, I've wondered what brought Frank here. Was it this Hobart Hanson?"

"I don't know. I don't know how he could have learned where Hanson was holing in. Frank wouldn't be the type he'd confide in. Yet if they're both here—"

"And, Dan, do you remember when he first came how he tried to pump me about writers?"

Smith roared with laughter as Adrienne realized what she'd revealed. "Now I know I'm on the right track," he said. "I'll let you in on this. My tip came from a reader . . . a manuscript reader for a crime magazine. One Hobart Hanson submitted the story of this particular bank robbery with such accuracy only one on the inside could have written it.

"The story was so well done the magazine bought the story. As you know, stories aren't published for some six months after purchase. That

159

meant Hanson was safe in this one spot for that long. Now what are you thinking?"

"Estimating time. He's still safe."

Or was he planning to leave?

"Dan, why didn't you have your mail come to The Oaks?"

"Precautionary. The post office was too small. A chance remark could have alerted our Mr. Hanson, who'd have been listening."

"You followed him to Tarryville, didn't you?"

"I spotted a likely suspect, but you threw me off, you and the townspeople. I was told he was a well known rancher who'd been there for years."

Adrienne nodded. "Most of the people in that town are new. It's a mushroom town."

Fortunately for Adrienne's nerves, Collier arried. Dan left them alone together, and Adrienne told him the package she'd broken had been hair dye. Remembering she'd never seen Hanson without a knitted cap, except the one time in Tarryville, she'd begun to associate him with a badly mutilated circular on their wall.

From questions Dan had asked, she had felt he would have a clear picture and had gone to him. Now she knew Hobart Hanson, the writer, was the post office and bank robber.

Dan was called in, and now Adrienne could really talk. She could tell how she had noticed the times he came in for mail, early morning or late evening during the months of late and early darkness; how he'd complained of a bad ankle on his last trip and she had brought the mail out to him.

They told her then to run down and have her dinner. Resentfully she left, yet she could understand their reasoning. Hanson might not be an easy man to capture. The less she was involved, the safer for her.

She wasn't hungry; she was excited. When Rod came to her table, she looked up, eyes shining, longing to tell him.

"You look as though something pretty wonderful had happened," he said soberly.

"It has, Rod, but I can't tell you yet."

"Congratulations," he remarked, wheeled and walked off.

Now how does he know, she wondered, and why is he upset about it? Men! She'd never understand them, any of them.

The excitement died and boredom set in. Of all nights for Caroline to have a date. She, Adrienne, could not even have the room she had taken in lieu of the whole house, half of which belonged to her. Would nothing ever be settled?

Her boredom didn't last long. Frank Van de Mark came into the lounge. At first glance Adrienne wondered how she had ever seen anything good-looking about him. Now his features seemed frozen to a mask. Only his eyes were alive, and if ever hatred was a living thing, those eyes expressed it.

"Outside," he ordered.

"I'm not moving out," she informed him. "I'm tired of being badgered by you."

"You'll be a lot more tired if you don't. Where's Nolga?"

She looked at him in surprise and puzzlement. "You know as well as I do. It was you who insisted I not even speak to her on the telephone."

"You really don't know? Well, she's not at the hospital. You do know that."

Really frightened, Adrienne cried, "Oh, but, Frank, she must be. I talked to the ward nurse this morning."

"I went you one better. I got a line on a nice bit of kitchen help. She told me Mrs. Akars had been taken away from the hospital yesterday. Hey, where you going?"

She was going to a lobby telephone booth. But when she sought to close the door, Frank's foot was there.

"Having trouble, Addie?"

Rod Burrows had come up. Now he looked at Van de Mark, and Frank stepped back. "It's nothing. I got a tip my fiancée had been shanghaied out of the hospital. Adrienne was just trying to locate her for me."

"Why not come up to my office, Addie?" Rod suggested. "Be more comfortable if you've more than one call to make."

"Good idea. Too public here," Frank agreed.

"You were not included," Rod told him, and steered Adrienne toward the elevator.

"I'll talk to you later," Frank said, with a meaning Adrienne understood.

When they reached Rod's office he locked the other door, then went through to his room. But she called him back. "I don't mind you listening. I've an idea Frank pestered them so at the hospital, Dr. Angel had her moved elsewhere."

Dr. Angel almost confirmed that. He told Adrienne it had seemed advisable to move her to a place more easily guarded against unwelcome visitors. It might be better if she, Adrienne, didn't know where.

"Addie," Rod spoke when she relayed the doctor's words, "why are you putting up with Frank, letting him use your home, letting him keep you upset?"

"The house is half Nolga's, Rod. And thus far Frank has done nothing but badger; there's no law against that. But I'm glad I am living here at the hotel."

"Dan should take better care of you."

"Dan?" she asked in surprise. "Why should he—" And then she stopped. Now she understood why Rod had offered congratulations. And she couldn't tell him the truth.

"I wish Jones would get back to town. I don't know where he comes into this deal, but the company's getting anxious. I can't hold off much longer. I wouldn't for anyone but you, Addie. I'd like to see you free of a lot of things."

"Then you have other land in mind?"

"We always have. We prefer yours, but time is important. We'd like to start building."

Adrienne put her elbows on the desk, her head in her hands. If Rod's company bought other land, Jones wouldn't want the Akars land, either. They'd be right back where they were, with seven more years to serve. She couldn't face it.

Finally she lifted her head. "Please wait a little longer, Rod. I asked Craig to investigate something for me."

"Why Craig?" he asked bluntly.

Yes, why Craig? Suddenly she saw the purpose of her request as he might see it, to bring about an exposé of Nolga which would turn him against her. She hadn't meant it that way. She wasn't trying to force him to release Nolga's signature on his agreement by any such underhanded method.

"I'm beginning to wonder," she replied. "It seemed like a good idea at the time."

She started for the door, then turned back and asked if she might make a house call. She was really a woman without a home for a little while.

"Don't go," she said when he started out and she had given her room number. "Oh, Dan, Frank's in the lobby and I'm in Rod's office. Oh, I'll ask him."

She turned to the man who stood, his face

164

square, each line unrelenting. "Rod, Dan wants to know if he can hold a conference here. Mr. Collier and some other men are with him. Their need for privacy is—"

"Addie, is this—" Suddenly he looked different, as though some load had been lifted. "I mean Dan, Collier, your looking excited and these other men. Great guns, yes, girl. Tell them to come on, and I personally will escort you back and look under the bed."

"You and your IBM mind," she chided.

He couldn't say much more. They found a completely bewildered Caroline wandering along the corridor.

"What on earth's going on? It sounds as if a hive of bees got into our room."

"Bees don't smoke cigars," Rod told her, sniffing the air.

"What was Frank doing up here? He sneaked up the stairs just after I took the elevator," Caroline reported. "When I told him I was calling the house detective, he really steamed back down."

"I'll go down and keep him company," Rod said. "Nothing I'd enjoy better in my own sweet way. What am I to tell him about Mrs. Akars?"

Adrienne sighed. "Let me think of some four-bit words he won't grasp. Tell him Dr. Angel diagnosed Nolga's illness as psychosomatic and sent her to a private sanatorium for therapy. You might add a speedy recovery is indicated."

"Why that?" asked Caroline after Rod had saluted and left.

"To hold him here where he can be watched instead of out bribing the hospital help in an attempt to locate her."

"Oh, to be a Nolga," crooned Caroline. "She knows just when to faint. You should try it sometime."

"Me they'd throw water on."

Adrienne slept well for some reason. She took pains with her dressing because of the suit Gypsy had literally rebuilt. Originally a "washed out blue" Nolga wouldn't be caught "dead in," Gypsy had added reveres, waistcoat and cuffs of pink and blue stripes that gave it a festive air.

Caroline was also bursting into bloom in one of her discards that had suffered a Gypsy change.

"My word," she breathed as they came out of the elevator, "men! Look at them. And good-looking. Salesmen. Now what is there at The Oaks to bring such prime specimens?"

They were seated at a window table when Caroline looked up again. "Imagine, two jackpots in a row. But these didn't register; they came straight in. Fishermen."

"Mind forgetting you saw any of them?" asked Adrienne.

"Something to do with the smoke-filled room?"

"I think so."

"Well, look, Addie dear, if I burst with curiosity, just pick up the pieces and label them, 'Living with Addie.' "

"Think how maddening it is for me," Adrienne pleaded. "I don't know half as much as I'm supposed to know. Let's hope things clear up before I crack up."

"Don't look now, but here comes a cloud that will need clearing."

Adrienne looked up and saw Craig Jones, still in topcoat and hat, heading for her table. "What have you done with Nolga?" he demanded.

"I love you, too," Adrienne retorted.

"I went to the hospital; they said she'd been moved. Came over here and found that Van de Mark at your house, living there! He said you were here, that you'd gotten rid of Nolga so she couldn't go through with our deal."

"For goodness sakes sit down before they call the militia to quell you," ordered Caroline. "You have everybody in the room staring."

Craig stared around, stared at Addie. "Where did all these men come from?"

"News of our charm got out," Caroline replied. "Will you either sit down or leave? Addie, snap out of it."

"I'm sorry, Craig; do sit down. Dr. Angel had Nolga moved because, unless he kept a police guard handy, he didn't know if he could keep Frank away from her. I didn't know she'd been moved until he told me. I was glad. Dan Smith managed a run-down on Frank."

That caught his attention. He drew out a chair, barked, "Coffee," at the hovering waiter, and turned to Adrienne.

"He found what he expected," Adrienne told him. "Just a very small time confidence man. Only one minor conviction against him. I imagine from what Dan says, he only pries money from women who are too proud to prosecute him publicly."

"Yet you let him live in Nolga's house."

"Steady on," murmured Caroline. "That's half Adrienne's, but it's Nolga's half he's taken over."

"Craig, I have to hurry to work. Please let me know what you've learned, if anything?"

"I'll drive you there; then I'm going down to your house and boot that woman-worrier out."

When Adrienne parted from Caroline she gave her a pat in lieu of the information her friend was yearning to receive, then picking up her coat, joined Craig.

"I found out what Frank was holding over Nolga," Craig began abruptly. "A previous marriage with no divorce."

Adrienne swung to look at him. Then Nolga wasn't Mrs. Akars after all.

Chapter Fifteen

"Well, say something," snapped Craig.

"Oh, poor Nolga," cried Adrienne obediently. "Craig, there's some mistake some place. I know Nolga can be trying and rattlebrained and—"

"I know; go on."

"But she's too inherently decent to have married my father without believing she was free. We've got to *do* something, Craig. Can't divorce be made retroactive or something?"

"You mean you *want* her to inherit the half due Mrs. Akars?"

"If she doesn't, I'll certainly give her that half."

"I'd just as soon you didn't, Addie. I want to marry her if she'll have me. After this deal with Frank, she's going to be suspicious of fortune hunters. However," he pulled the car up before the post office, "you needn't worry. Nolga didn't get a divorce, but her aunt had that marriage annulled."

Adrienne looked at him in complete exasperation. "If you knew the strain I'd been under you wouldn't do things like this. Now tell me about it. Whom did she marry and when, and if the aunt got the annulment—"

"She was under age; sixteen, to be exact. There was an air base—since closed—not too far from her home town. Nolga met this fellow, who gave her quite a rush, and one day they eloped.

"It took the aunt two weeks to find her. In fact, it was the military who located the couple; the young fellow was AWOL. In the meantime Mrs. Knudsen, the aunt, had gone into a thorough investigation of the man. He had been in and out of reform schools, had all the makings of a Grade-A criminal.

"This chap was transferred out soon afterwards, fortunately. Nolga had built him up in her mind as persecuted. A few years and she was grateful to her aunt for saving her. She left the small town and went to business school and then began working."

"How did she ever get this far north?" Adrienne wondered.

"Mrs. Knudsen says it must have been because of a subconscious desire to get away from the scene of her big mistake."

Adrienne nodded.

"Craig, what I don't understand is why she let Frank frighten her. If the marriage had been annulled, she had nothing to worry about."

"That," he sighed, "is why I'm trying to find her. From a chance remark of Frank's, it's possible he convinced her there was a fault in the annulment."

Adrienne shook her head. "It's more than that. I know Nolga. When she's done something wrong, or something that seems wrong and isn't her fault, she turns into a little child and throws herself on your mercy. I've had that happen so many times I know it's instinctive."

She had to go to the post office. As they talked she had been aware of the salesmen parking their cars at strategic spots, her nerves tightening with each evidence of what might be ahead.

"I'll see you this evening," he promised. "I'll talk to the Judge and have him talk to the doctor."

Absently Adrienne nodded and left. Craig had won and she had make his victory possible by sending him to investigate Nolga's background.

Now Rod would have to buy the other land. His company couldn't let this fine weather slip past. Craig had said he wanted to marry Nolga. Adrienne, knowing Nolga, knew she would literally leap into the arms of a protector, especially one able to take care of her financially.

When she went in, Collier briefed her. Insofar as she could, she had given a pattern of Hobart Hanson's trips to the post office. When he'd first arrived they had been more or less regular. Of late they hadn't.

"But he'll want the hair dye," she told them. "He can't keep on wearing those caps much longer."

Her mind went on with her own problem as she

sheafed through letters. Nolga would naturally insist upon selling to Craig. If Craig didn't in turn sell to Ewa at their figure, Ewa would buy elsewhere and Rod would disappear from her life.

Yet if Ewa bought elsewhere, just what could that land mean to Craig's company?

Adrienne knelt down and scooped up a letter she'd dropped. Imagine, after all of these years, dropping things. However—she brightened—that one drop had paid off.

Rod chose a moment when the foyer was empty to come in after his mail. Stopping at the window, he said fiercely, "Why don't you have a nervous breakdown?"

"Give me time," she returned. "Another month like this last one—"

He tried to join in her humorous approach. "You might break a leg—"

"Couldn't you think of something less painful?"

Rod gave up then. "Perhaps I thought that would be. Addie, will you have lunch with me?"

"If you don't mind the counter next door. I can't leave today."

"Then dinner?"

"I'd like to. But you must not worry if Craig comes in. I think he's going to have a message for me from Nolga."

And, she thought unhappily, I'll have a message for Ewa.

Colier kept Adrienne until a late lunch hour.

Tessie had been replaced by a male clerk who went carefully over the few pieces of mail in Hobart Hanson's box: a returned manuscript; a folder from a correspondence school in writing.

Adrienne had noted that in particular. Hanson's one sale had been made because he had known his subject, not because of his writing ability.

"Why did he expose himself that way?" she asked the new clerk.

"It's a form of megalomania criminals of his type suffer. He pulled off what to him was a brilliant robbery. He even got away from the two working with him, carrying the money with him. But he had no immediate audience. There was no one to tell him what a great and wonderful mind he had."

"Oh," Adrienne was remembering, "when he picked up returned manuscripts he always had a smarter-than-thou look, as though he were scorning the editors who hadn't sense enough to know he knew more about the subject than they."

"Right. Winter is a hard time to hole up. I imagine he began cracking soon after the first of the year and decided to write his masterpiece, the story of his own big robbery. We haven't had time to check with the magazine, but I'm sure when we do we'll find the story wasn't purchased for its literary value but for its force, its authority."

173

She referred to Hanson once again. "I really don't expect him until the next storm."

"One due in over the weekend; supposed to strike Sunday night. We're keeping track because of the boys in the hills."

Adrienne glanced at the calendar and gave a sigh of relief. Monday fell on the twenty-eighth. There would be few people in the post office, and none of the older ones.

At one o'clock Adrienne went to the coffee shop. Dan Smith picked up his lunch platter on the counter and brought it over to her booth.

"News," he reported, "but not good. Little Frankie has departed bag and baggage. He's left an unholy mess behind. Let me call that couple Nolga had in."

"But why isn't that good?" Adrienne cried. "You need your room, and I'm running out of clothes and things."

"He's running out of money and can't reach Nolga. We're pretty sure he had some lead on Hanson possibly through Hanson's girl friend that brought him here. He would know that Hanson had the money cached near where he was holing in.

"Frank gets around. He knows the town well. An influx of men would make him curious. I've known his kind to say they could 'smell a cop.'

"So Frank, up early this morning because Craig came roaring in, senses something is going on. Because he's on the lookout for Hanson, he reasons, so are the others.

"I'm willing to bet he's trying to reach Hanson first to trade information for cash money, just as he'd have used some other angle to get money from Hanson if he had spotted him here. He didn't spot him. He met Nolga at the hotel in the meantime and found her easy pickings. Then came the chance for Belmont to buy the Akars place for thirty-two thousand. If by blackmailing Nolga he could get his hands on a good part of that, he wouldn't risk what he'd risk facing Hanson. That, he now knows, fell through."

"Oh, but—"

"I mean he knows he can't reach Nolga in time. I happen to know he owes a bill at the inn and over at the garage. And I imagine around Lakeville there are a few others. They're closing in on him. What's worse in his lexicon, his car isn't paid for and the company carrying the papers is ready to pick it up."

Adrienne shuddered.

"Addie," Dan was serious, "where did I slip up on Hanson?"

She thought back to the two times the man had been in for his mail. "I don't think you did. He came in the evening you arrived just before we closed. The next time he was there an hour before opening and had me bring his mail out to him. Like a fool, I did."

"And Tarryville?"

Adrienne recalled. "At first glance I identified the man as Hanson, but after a moment I wasn't sure. Now I know it was because of his clothes and the cap he wore."

"And your refusal to let anything having to do with post office business surprise you into speaking. Anyhow, I feel better."

He stood up, said he'd send someone after the Larsons. If she wanted to return home, fine. But she should know she had an uncle visiting her.

"Uncle? Oh, well, let me know his name."

Having a half-hour before she needed to return to the post office, Adrienne hurried down the lane toward home. She felt she'd been away for months instead of days and was surprised to find no great change.

Lilac buds were forming but still folded tight in deep purple coats, the ranaculas splashed flower borders, and anenomes still bloomed. Forsythia still tossed golden bells, but less gold than when she had left.

Just outside the garage Adrienne spied a mound of something and, investigating, found it composed of tin cans. Frank would never starve as long as he had a can opener and could beg, borrow or steal a can of food to which to apply it.

Stepping into the house, Adrienne waited a moment. There was a strange chill in the place, an unused, deserted air.

Ridiculous, she thought, and went on in to find Frank had lived in the kitchen and small dining ell.

Again she paused and listened. If the Larsons weren't available and she intended to sleep there that night, she'd better run up and open windows.

Adrienne laughed a little as she caught herself tiptoeing. She didn't scream when Nolga appeared suddenly before her; instead she froze.

Nolga was mouthing some word. Adrienne found herself straining to catch it, feeling somehow she'd been caught up in a dream, a nightmare. She tried to walk and found herself approaching her stepmother, shocked at her appearance, the deathly whiteness of her face, the dark-rimmed eyes.

And then the word came out. "Run!" And fast after that, "Run, Addie, run back—"

"I wouldn't," remarked a smooth voice. "Just walk forward, in here. Nolga, back in with you, too. Frank, take care of her."

"Mr. Hanson," Adrienne found her voice, "imagine seeing you here."

"Just looking after my rights, Miss Akars. My wife, you know, ran out on me some time ago. Took me a little while to locate her, but I did. Now if you'll come in quietly, we'll settle this in a way to benefit all of us."

"Your wife?"

Hobart Hanson smiled grimly. "Yes, my child

bride of quite a number of years ago. She had me picked up and thrown in, you know. I haven't forgotten. Now she's going to help to keep me from being thrown in again."

Adrienne shook her head as though to free it of some fantasy. This was her own home, this upper hall the place where she had played on rainy days as a child; that small bay window the place where she'd sat reading and watching for her Dad to come down the lane from the post office.

Adrienne moved into Nolga's room to find Frank standing behind Nolga's chair, smoking nervously; Frank, whom Craig Jones had said had left, bag and baggage, hours ago.

"So you came back," Adrienne observed.

"On my orders," Hanson answered her pleasantly.

"My car—the company took it," Frank managed.

"And I don't care to drive my jeep just now. Nothing bullet-proof about a jeep; ever notice that, Miss Akars? However, my wife has a car. We want that, and we want it filled with gas and driven to a spot where we can pick it up without an audience, understand?"

Adrienne found it advisable to understand. The rundown she'd had on Hanson's character seemed accurate. He was a great man in his own estimation and about to bring off another brilliant coup.

"We're in a very neat position here," Hanson

picked up his monologue, "upstairs, with little Nolga as a safeguard. A stairway is very easy to guard, and we have plenty of ammunition.

"Nolga, running true to character, didn't stop to check the gas tank. Her car is down the road some distance. She walked in."

"I came home the minute I heard *he* was gone," Nolga managed before Frank slapped a hand over her mouth.

It wasn't a wise move. Nolga bit, Frank yelled, and Hanson wasted a moment or two quelling him; moments Adrienne used to evaluate their position. But it was useless. Hanson had out-plotted her.

"First you will call your post office," he resumed. "Tell your boss you're going after your car and will be late getting back. You inconvenienced us there, Miss Akars; we didn't expect you before evening.

"Next you will call a garage, have them pick you up at the lane and carry gasoline to the car. When the garage car leaves, you will drive my wife's car down that road which cuts through to the beach. Understand?"

Adrienne nodded.

"We will hold the little woman. If you go wrong any place—"

"He means," Frank spoke in a high, nervous voice, "if we've got to shoot it out here we'll put her in front, understand?"

Adrienne smiled at Hanson. "Nice plotting."

She thought, once they're away I can call. They can be stopped at Lakeville or Tarryville.

"We will take Nolga with us," Hanson went on pleasantly, "to forestall any effort to stop us. Now, ready to make your first call?"

"Oh, my," Adrienne's voice lifted, "the Larsons. Mr. Smith was going to get them over to clean up. Frank left the kitchen in such a mess—"

"You slob!" For the first time the tautness of Hanson's nerves cut through to his voice as he turned on Frank. Then he wheeled back to Adrienne. "Can you stop them?"

"I can try."

They ran down to the telephone to put the call through. Adrienne left word that a friend had cleaned up, that the Larsons weren't needed. "We can hang a sign on the door, too," she offered, hoping "the visiting uncle" wouldn't be the one to bring them.

Hanson stood where he could watch her face when she called Collier.

"Addie," Collier asked, alarmed, "are you all right?"

"I'm sorry," she apologized. "This strain has made me sound nervous, as well as drop mail and break bottles. And Nolga looks so worn out. I'll bring her car home, then be over. Okay?"

"Fine. I'll have the wife give you a prescription for her nerve medicine. Made a new *man* of Tessie."

180

Hanson heard and thought nothing of what was said. He stood by until the garage car came, then gave her a last warning.

"Just one slip-up and you'll be the one to blame for Nolga's death. I mean it, Miss Akars."

"I know you do," Adrienne replied wearily.

The driver of the car was not the garage man. As quickly as she could Adrienne told him of Hanson's plan, then asked how he'd chanced to be there.

"The broken bottle you mentioned to Collier. Now to plan how we can catch them off base. There's a state police car waiting out of sight beyond Mrs. Akar's car; they'll radio back."

The police car pulled in beside them. Adrienne was frantically aware of strong binoculars trained on them from the high windows of the Akars house.

Swiftly the driver told the officer the set-up; then they heard a squawk as the radio came on.

"Someone just fell out a second floor window of the Akars place. A woman!"

Chapter Sixteen

"Can you make it?" asked the anxious voice of the garage car driver.

"I have to," Adrienne replied in a dead voice.

"They'll start heading for the car as soon as you turn in on the orchard road. Don't go too far. If you can drive the car to cover, get out of there as fast as you can."

"Yes sir," whispered Adrienne.

Nolga had fallen from a second floor window. The bedroom window? Cement below. Poor Nolga. But how had she managed to get the window open with those two men in the room? Maybe they'd thrown her. No, they needed her.

Suddenly Adrienne was angry. "Wouldn't she do a thing like that? I could wring her—" She stopped there and swallowed. She couldn't say the word.

One mile, a mile and a half. And she'd thought this car fast.

"You all right?" asked an anxious voice behind her.

"I think so. I turn here; you boys brace yourselves."

Into the lane that led through the orchard to an old barn she'd once thought of turning into a studio. Grain had formerly been kept there.

"Apples," she said aloud. "I mean the old barn smelled like apples in the winter."

Thank goodness the trees had leafed out a little. And the ground was good and soft; if she drove off and the others did get into the car, they'd never get out in time.

At the last clear place Adrienne looked toward the house. Something had caught her attention. Something was hanging from the bathroom window—sheets tied together.

"I'll buy her a dozen coral-colored sweaters," she announced. "Stay steady; I'm going into the mud."

She opened the car door, waited for the men in back to ease out, then got out slowly, following instructions to go back and look at a rear tire.

"They're coming out of a shed off that barn," announced one man. "Now get ready; duck behind!"

Adrienne did more than duck. She rolled behind the car, wishing the mud could cover her, as a fusillade of shots rang out.

Something covered her, a protective bulk of a man. And when triumphant shouts rang out ahead, Adrienne tried to unscrew her eyelids enough to look up.

"Why, Rod," she said, and fainted.

But when she opened her eyes it was Nolga who was holding her.

"Oh," murmured Adrienne, "so you didn't break your neck."

"I wish I had," moaned Nolga. "I almost cost you your life. I don't blame you for wanting—"

"I didn't. I even said I'd buy you a dozen sweaters."

"I think that's enough for now," observed a pleasant voice, and Adrienne turned her head to see Dr. Angel beside her.

"What are you doing here?"

"Someone thought a doctor was indicated. I came over to stand by in case of need."

"Were you?"

"Oh, yes. One has a shattered gun hand, the other a hole in his tummy. Won't be cadging meals for a little while. Might even reform. We shipped them off. You're all right; just need a little rest."

Now Adrienne lifted her head a little. Ah, there he was, standing over in the corner of the room looking "square."

"You might like to talk her to sleep, Mr. Burrows," suggested the doctor. "Now, Mrs. Akars, let's look at those bruises."

Nothing Rod said made much sense at first, except for the statement that he loved her and he didn't care if she did sell to Craig. Ewa would just pay more to buy it back, and who cared as long as she was all right?

If she'd have him, he'd even buy this house from Jones for her.

"I don't think I want it," murmured Adrienne. "I'd always think of that upper hall and how I felt talking to Hanson."

"Well, that's good. Nolga wants it for the same reason. She said whenever she felt herself getting out of hand, she'd go upstairs and remember how you'd stood up to those men, were ready to sacrifice yourslf for her."

"Oh, I was in no danger."

"Oh, yes, you were, and you knew it. Now—"

"Rod, how did she fall out of the wondow?"

He stammered a little. "Seems someone walked up to the front door, and the two men were so busy watching she chose that time to say she was going to the bathroom. Frank stood guard. But she'd grabbed up his 'filthy' sheets. Inside, she bolted the door, tied them together, tied one end to a towel rack and went out the window—too fast. She screamed, and I got there in time to break the fall. The towel rack had come with her."

"Just like Nolga. Rod, why did you go to the front door?"

"Someone had to distract them while the men took position around the barn and sheds, didn't he? Frank knew me—"

"How did you know Frank was there?"

185

"The fellow who picked up his car for the mortgage company saw him heading back there. We figured he had a key. He'd be the type who'd have an extra one made."

"Then how did he contact Hanson?"

"Hanson contacted him. Let's back-track. When the two were serving sentences for some minor crimes some time ago, they became acquainted. Hanson's a great braggart. Among other things he told Frank about his wife, Nolga. He'd always been furious, evidently, because the marriage was annulled. But of course he'd never admit an annulment to another man."

"So he told Frank," Adrienne picked up the story, "that the girl's aunt had thought she'd got a divorce, but as he'd never been served, it wasn't final. He also told him he'd kept track of her. She was now the widow of a wealthy man. He intended going after her one of these days."

"Then when Frank read of the robbery and identified Hanson, he remembered and came looking. Why did he look for a writer?"

"That same bruised ego. Some newspaperman who was making a name for himself by writing true crime stories had written a news story about Hanson, calling him a punk of some kind. Hanson had sworn to Frank that some day he'd pick up a swag, hole in and write for the same magazine; write something better."

Adrienne waited a minute. "How did you learn

all of this in such a short time, and Frank with a hole in his stomach?"

"Doctor was there with the hypo, and Frankie, thinking he was going to die, told all."

"Now, Rod, let's go back to you coming to the house. Why you?"

"I was the one person Frank wouldn't suspect of being interested in him or in Hanson. I was ready to do anything. I planned to walk casually up to the front door, do a lot of bell ringing, then, under shelter of the wall, sneak around to where I could run interference when you drove in.

"Nolga literally played into my hands—"

"And Nolga," the brisk woman coming in with a tray bore no resemblance to the hollow-eyed woman Adrienne had seen earlier that day, "is now going to run you out. Here, Adrienne, warm milk and a long nap. You and Rod have the rest of your lives—" She stopped and looked distraught. "You do plan to, don't you? Spend the rest of your lives together?"

"I do!" they chanted in solemn unison.

"And in the marriage ceremony," stated Rod, "shall be inserted a clause: 'No extracurricular activities without the husband's knowledge.'

"I'll see you when you wake up," he added, leaving.

"Where's Caroline?" Adrienne asked, longing to share this moment with her friend.

"Oh, sitting with her nose glued to the window,

waiting for Dan. Addie, do you mind if I borrow that new print of yours? Craig—"

Nolga stopped to stare at Adrienne, who was laughing hysterically. "Here, quick, the milk and this pill. Whatever is funny?"

"The whole world," Adrienne managed. "And how much of it will I miss if I take the pill?"

"Enough for Gypsy to finish a creation she thought up. You really should look your best upon becoming engaged, you know."

Dutifully Adrienne swallowed, then leaned back with a great sigh. The strain was over. Well, most. At least Rod loved her; nothing much mattered but that.

She looked around the big master bedroom. The small stove sizzled and crackled, or the wood therein. Maybe she shouldn't have been so quick to say she didn't want this for her home.

This is the Akars place, she reasoned sleepily, and tried to see herself and Rod there. No, it isn't, she decided. This has always been the home of the postmaster, who was an Akars. That era is past. Oh, my goodness, I have to go to work in the morning.

The mail had long since been distributed and picked up when Adrienne awoke. For a moment she lay remembering, and it was like the rising of the sun after months of storm.

"Awake?"

Eyes wide, Adrienne stared. Gypsy Duncan

stood there, something warm and rosy and lovely hanging from her hand.

"They're waiting for breakfast with you. Up and at them; I'll do your hair."

"Who's they?" Adrienne asked, coming out from a quick shower to let Gypsy turn her into a radiant being.

"Judge and Mrs. Cobb, Jones and Smith and Caroline and Nolga. And Rod Burrows is expected at any moment. He had to go to Lakeville to pick up something he ordered last week."

Conscious she had never looked lovelier, Adrienne went down the hall, to stop at the door of the dining ell. The table was set as for a party, and grouped around it were all of the people she loved the most.

Rod was standing waiting for her. When she entered with Gypsy, Craig stood up, too.

"This is an announcement breakfast, Addie," he said soberly, "and I'm master of ceremonies."

He waited until the three were seated and had greeted the Judge and his wife.

"The reason I was away so long," he continued, "was because I was taking time to go to company headquarters. I was resigning. It was one thing to buy up land for them to promote, quite another to deprive the woman I loved of her true profit in her inheritance.

"Nolga and I have talked it out. She's ready to sell to Ewa. We're going to try to make some agreement with Ewa to give us land instead of money."

Adrienne's mouth flew open. Nolga wanted land instead of money?

"I doubt if the company wants the lake front. I could build a fine tract of homes there. Of course we'll have to find some way to gain clear title; perhaps a will contest which I will subsidize—"

"Wait," rapped Judge Cobb. "You intend to marry Nolga soon?"

"Just as quickly as she'll have me."

"If you file before noon today you can marry Monday. We can hold up negotiations until after the ceremony, and then you won't need a will contest."

The judge beamed on the party. "Mr. Akars had a secret clause in his will. If at any reasonable time after his death his widow should remarry, the estate could be settled. He had no desire to work a hardship on either Mrs. Akars or upon Adrienne by forcing her to live under the same roof with the new husband."

"So that—" cried Adrienne, then stopped. That was why he had wanted her to marry Frank Van de Mark, to marry anyone. But then the Judge did not know Nolga as well as she.

"Now, Burrows, is this all right with you?"

"Yes, but we can't very well be married Monday," he replied absently. "I've wires here from home. My mother would like to be present. I called her last night," he explained to Adrienne seriously, then became aware everyone was laughign. "Oh, you mean about Ewa. Of course it's what we'd hope might happen."

"Oh, dear," cried Nolga, "Monday. I'll have to shop this afternoon."

"No, you won't," interposed Craig smoothly. "You haven't any cash. You owe me five hundred and you have too many clothes already. Wear them out. We're going to need capital to get our tract going. I'm not made of money."

Nolga's face crumpled, then straightened, and Adrienne understood. Now that Nolga knew she was loved, she didn't have to dress up the exterior to attract someone.

"Oh, well, I'll be busy preparing for Addie's wedding. Caroline, you'll be bridesmaid, won't you?"

"Bridesmaid." Dan had come in. "Then Addie can be matron of honor when school's out. I have to leave tomorrow night, but I'll take a real vacation in June."

Someone asked what Adrienne was looking for. She didn't tell them. She waited until she and Rod, with the flimsy excuse that they had to send telegrams, had driven toward Lakeville, then parked on a headland looking up the lake.

"Nolga and Craig, Caroline and Dan, and you and I. For the first time there isn't a man too many."

Clouds, forerunners of the storm due to strike the next day, rolled over the mountains, darkening the lake. Adrienne snuggled more closely into the warm embrasure of Rod's arm. Let the storm strike now.

"Addie, just one question. Remember the talk we had about you and your sister? You sort of let me know you'd changed because of some man."

"Umhum, a man who looked at me and didn't see me. I guess, Rod, many of them had. But I didn't care until the one man who mattered came to the window."